Citadel 32: A Tale

By Tom Merritt

Copyright

Citadel 32: A Tale of the Aggregate
by Tom Merritt
Creative Commons © 2015 Tom Merritt
Printed in the United States of America

This book is licensed under the Creative Commons Attribution-NonCommercial-ShareAlike 3.0 License.
http://creativecommons.org/licenses/by-nc-sa/3.0/us/
NOTES:
This story was written as part of the National Novel Writing Month movement, November 2012.

ISBN: 978-1-312-94592-0

Dedication

To: Grandma Adele.

All those World Almanacs you bought me paid off.

Acknowledgements:

Thanks to NaNoWriMo as always for pushing me to write.

Thanks to C.J. Harrison who always puts up with my frustratingly ridiculous artificial and contradictory worlds and somehow manages to help me make it better.

Thanks to Scott Johnson for the AMAZING cover art. He never ceases to blow me away with his talent and creativity.

Thanks to my wife, Eileen for never discouraging me and always doing something that makes me smile.

CHAPTER 1

Corge lay on his bunk watching sugar rock form on the wall. Novelties were scarce in Armstrong Station, so casually guessing what caused sugar rock was something of a national pastime. Its existence was a recent and so far unexplained phenomenon. A perfect distraction for Armstrong's residents, most of whom were descended from scientists. And distractions were at a premium. They focused so much energy on surviving, they had little left for anything else.

Corge usually spent his 30 minutes of downtime this way. Sugar rock got its name from the shiny look it gave rock, as if someone had sugar-glazed it. Once it appeared, you couldn't wipe it off. It wasn't a deposit. You couldn't chisel it away unless you chiseled off the underlying rock too. The small number of materials tests anyone had done showed it was composed of the same elements as the rock walls. Sometimes it disappeared without a trace. Corge looked at this new example on his wall. He was sort of glad to see it. Sugar rock appeared unpredictably, and he hadn't had an example to stare at in days.

Before inspiration struck and revealed to him the secrets of sugar rock, a buzzer warned him he needed to get back to work. Armstrong itself never rested—and its citizens never rested long. He struggled to his feet, stretched, ducked his head and stepped through the small portal that led out of his bunk-sized room.

A third of the dome was changing shifts, so the corridors were busy. For Armstrong, "busy" meant Corge could see more than two or three people at once. He nodded to a few folks and headed toward the ventilation shafts to get back to work on clearances. Ugh.

Corge was a Utility class worker, meaning he never worked the same job for long, but he hated working clearances for any amount of time. It was the worst. He absolutely could not wait to get upgraded to Generalist, as long as he didn't get assigned clearances as his primary area. He didn't get to choose that, of course. The Executives did. He could appeal their decision, but they rarely changed one. It would hardly be worth the hassle, unless they gave him clearances.

Corge found Tracy waiting at the top of Vent Shaft 5. Tracy was an Apprentice, on the verge of being promoted to Utility. She had a little swagger these days, so he guessed she knew it was coming. She shouldn't worry in any case. You had to be useless not to get promoted from Apprentice. You always got promoted and usually to Utility. If you were a washout, you got "promoted" to Tender. Poor Tenders. Some argued that Tenders didn't mind being Tenders, but that sounded a little too *Brave New World* for Corge's taste.

"She's down at the second bend," said Tracy before he asked. "I'm waiting for a torch-head replacement."

"She busted it?" he asked.

"Nah, but she didn't want to waste time when she did, so she called for it already."

He shook his head. LeAnn was the quintessential Specialist, almost too perfect at her job. He wondered if he'd ever reach her level of perfectionism. Most folks leveled out at Generalist, being pretty good at a few things and taking pride in those. There was no shame in that. Specialists were a different breed. They were consumed with talent for one thing—and they excelled at it.

He saw flickering light from around the corner before he saw LeAnn. She was using a photon welder that gave off no sound or heat but mended cracks without wasting resources. In a sealed community like Armstrong, that wasn't only important, it was life or death. Lots of things were life and death in Armstrong. LeAnn shut the torch down and the light faded as he walked up.

"You're not wearing your mask," LeAnn said through hers.

Corge hated the damned thing. It was really only necessary when vent shafts had air clearance issues. This was an integrity clearance. In other words, none of the cracks could expose them to vacuum. An emergency Specialist crew would have handled an air clearance, not Corge.

But LeAnn was a stickler for the rules, so he grabbed the thing hanging around his neck and shoved it up and over his face. "Better?" he mumbled.

LeAnn grunted. "Get on the fader and follow me down. I left you back about three meters, but you should catch up to me by the time I'm done. We're clearing cracks down to the corner—that's it."

He nodded and settled in for boredom. He didn't understand how LeAnn could be a Specialist at fixing cracks. She was so smart. So interesting. She had wild, fun thoughts and theories on all kinds of things, from ice finds to Executive politics to Earth. But somehow the powers that be determined her ultimate purpose was pointing a photon welder at microscopic rock cracks and preventing containment leaks in ventilation tunnels. The worst part, to Corge's way of thinking, was that they seemed to be right.

Corge drifted along with his work, thinking about a dinner he planned to make out of some protein variants he'd been hoarding. It wasn't really hoarding. Everybody was allowed a small amount of stockpiling in order to do just this sort of thing, as long as they contributed recipes back to the main kitchen. It was a way to keep the menus vibrant. He was thinking about how to ask LeAnn to try out his dinner creation when the ground shook.

Feeling the ground shake was the most frightening and horrible thing that could happen in Armstrong.

Without a word, LeAnn and Corge raced up the vent shaft to the main corridor. Tracy had already run to the nearest com port, but a crowd had beat her there and an older Generalist in Logistics was reading out the news to everyone.

"Unknown tremor from outside," he barked. "It's weird, folks. No internal explosion sensors. No accidents reported. It's like the ground just shook on its own."

"What did they used to call them on Earth—" a woman shouted, "earthquakes?"

"So this is a moonquake?" someone else blurted out.

"What else does it say?!" Corge yelled.

The man shook his head. "Nothing else so far. Emergency teams investigating. Stand by for action. DNR for now. We all stand around and burn air, I guess."

Corge had just turned to complain to LeAnn about the slow wheels of Armstrong bureaucracy when both their wrists buzzed.

"I'm needed in Central Control," LeAnn said without looking at him. "Wait here until the DNR lifts. I want to finish that vent shaft today if we can."

"Sorry, they want me in Central too," Corge answered.

LeAnn looked surprised, an unusual state for her, but she motioned for him to follow her. Like Corge didn't know the way to Central. Sometimes, he thought, Specialists could be a little too special for their own good.

CLASSES OF ARMSTRONG OCCUPATIONS
(An excerpt from the Database of Educational Records)

The Armstrong Occupational Track System (AOTS) was implemented shortly after Disconnection as a way to allocate resources effectively. At first, the system delineated three teams to which all residents were assigned: Science, Maintenance and Support. The system has been modified and expanded over time to become the more efficient and precise version now in use by the Executives. The AOTS system ensures that people can use their best talents to benefit Armstrong and keep its citizens alive until Disconnection ends. Described below are the available levels and opportunities and the system for making assignments.

> STUDENT – (Levels 1-12) Students can be employed in part-time tasks at the request of Specialists and with the approval of Executive committees.
>
> TRAINEE – Trainee is a one-year mandatory level for all residents completing the 12th Student level, Trainees fill service occupations in multiple departments.
>
> APPRENTICE – As the last nondiscretionary level, Apprentice assignments are made to multiple teams based on Trainee performance. Apprentices are similar to Trainees in type but with more responsibility. All Apprentices will be promoted to Tender or Utility.
>
> TENDER – Tenders conduct maintenance and service routines as assigned by the Executive Committee on Logistics. Prerequisite: Apprentice level.
>
> UTILITY – Apprentices or Tenders showing improvement are assigned to multiple teams. Utility workers are frequently evaluated for particular talents demonstrated at a high level. Prerequisite: Apprentice or Tender level.
>
> GENERALIST – The most populated level. Generalists are assigned to a limited number of teams, tailored to individual enjoyment and achievement but varied to ensure against burnout. Prerequisite: Utility level.
>
> SPECIALIST – Generalists who show an outstanding capacity for a particular task without signs of burnout will be promoted to Specialist in that category and receive leadership responsibility for those teams. Prerequisite: Generalist, or in special cases, Utility level.

EXECUTIVE – Generalists or Specialists who show broad leadership and management skills without signs of aggrandizement or antisocial behavior may be promoted to the Executive team for general coordination of Armstrong affairs. Pre-requisite: Generalist or Specialist level.

GOVERNANCE – The Governance Committee and its officers are predominantly elected from a pool of Executives and Specialists. Some positions are democratically elected; some are elected from within the ranks of a particular level as that level's representative. Officers are elected from within the Governance level itself. Prerequisite: Executive or Specialist level.

PATH TO PROMOTION

The Executive Committee on Education oversees assignments and path progression. This committee contains several Specialists in Education and Psychology.

STUDENT PROMOTION – Curriculum is set by a joint teacher-Executive board. Students who satisfy the curriculum standards are advanced. Students must advance or be treated for disorders.

NONSTUDENT PROMOTION – A joint Executive-Specialist committee is assembled to confer promotion on Apprentices and Generalists. Executives in charge of departments and teams chose when to promote Utility- or Tender-level residents based on performance and aptitude.

No appeal is allowed for nonpromotion except through the judicial system. Team assignments above the level of Utility can be appealed on the grounds that an individual knows their own preferences best and that personal preference is essential to good Generalists and Specialists.

Executive promotion can only be accepted or declined, not appealed. Only the Governance Committee of the whole in conjunction with the Educational Department can alter the system.

CHAPTER 2

Central Control occupied the hangar overlook in Docking Bay. A very old but very well-cared-for sign welcomed incoming visitors to "Armstrong Dome – Citadel 32." Armstrong was neither a dome nor a citadel. Although everyone still referred to "the dome." The base had actually been built in a subsurface lava tube bunker in the Mare Serenitatis. A temporary dome had existed in the early days of its construction but was dismantled long before Disconnection. On the other hand, almost nobody had ever called it one of the Citadels. It had been dubbed a Citadel politically as a nod to the great centers of power on Earth below. It never towered like a Citadel in either physical form or influence. But the sign remained. Sentimentality for such things was rare in Armstrong. When recycling and preserving every molecule was essential to your survival, you didn't get attached to material things. Docking Bay was the exception.

The idea that Earth might someday reawaken and return attention to its satellite never seemed impossible when you were in "The Bay." So the metal, paint and other materials that made up the sign were off limits for recycling except in the direst emergency. It was the last symbol of hope.

In fact, it was pretty much the only symbol left. No plaques marked the spot where station officers had informed the staff of the Disconnection so many years ago. The railing where they stood wasn't roped off or marked in any way. Corge put his hands all over it as he walked toward the door into the Central Control offices. Everybody did. It struck Corge that maybe that was the memorial, the touching of that spot. Sort of like touching a talisman.

These thoughts fled as he and LeAnn entered Central Control and sank into the buzzing noise that filled it. It seemed to be at a slightly more intense pitch than usual, which was saying something.

Executive Wenner waved them over to a bank of monitors. Wenner was a high-functioning math savant, one of the few Specialists who had transitioned to an Executive. He was a pattern recognizer. The Governance Committee found that invaluable in the station's constant battle against entropy, though his talents left little room for pleasantries or charm. As soon as Corge and LeAnn were in earshot, he began briefing them without any kind of greeting or introduction.

"First the rule-outs. No sensors indicate internal disturbance. It didn't come from inside the dome. Second, it doesn't have the characteristics of a seismic event." Here he chuckled. Snorted actually. "It shouldn't. There's no seismology on Luna. But it definitely has a man-made signature. Our best bet is some abandoned piece of tech out there." He waved in a random direction that meant "outside the dome." "Location pinpoints it nearest to Vent Shaft 5. What did you observe?"

Corge was still trying to piece together what Wenner was telling him when LeAnn answered.

"The crack patterns we were fixing showed no signs of fast action or other odd causes. They were all consistent with normal wear. Nothing unusual. The only thing significant was the length. They ran a bit farther up the shaft than this sort of wear normally does."

"How far?" snapped Wenner.

"I'd have to measure and research," LeAnn answered, knowing Wenner's insistence on precision. "But I'd guess a few meters over the average. Nothing outlandish."

Wenner smirked at this as if Corge and LeAnn had no idea what outlandish meant. Then he turned the smirk on Corge.

"What did you notice?"

Corge wasn't sure how to answer. "Well, I had just got back from break. I hadn't started working yet when the explosion happened."

"Disturbance. Shaking. Disruption. Not explosion. Explosion is much too precise. We don't know enough to call it an explosion. And we sure aren't going to figure it out if I don't get all the information, Corge. So stop worrying about what you think I'm going to think about what you say. Just tell me everything you noticed from the moment you arrived at the shaft. Don't leave anything out."

Corge sighed. He told Wenner everything he could think of from the moment he arrived and spoke to Tracy until the explos— disruption.

"What about Tracy? What was she doing when you arrived?" probed Wenner.

"Nothing really. Just standing there."

"In what manner?"

"What?"

"How," Wenner paused and just barely didn't roll his eyes, "was she standing there?"

"Normally? Relaxed. On two feet?" Corge couldn't figure out for the life of him what Wenner meant.

"Where was she looking?"

"At me."

"From the moment you saw her."

Corge had to think about that one. "Yeah. Yeah, I'm pretty sure. She was looking up the corridor for me. Saw me as soon as I came around the corner."

"Where were her hands? What were they doing?"

This was getting ridiculous. Corge wasn't a memetic. "I don't remember. At her sides, I think. I really don't recall."

"Good," Wenner seemed to relax at this. "What about during your break? What did you do? What did you see?"

Corge was certain his break wasn't relevant. His bunk was far from the vent shaft. But he was quickly figuring out Wenner wanted him to just answer anyway.

"I pretty much laid there thinking. I didn't run any progs or get on coms. Just laid there looking at the sugar rock on my wall."

"How long has the sugar rock been there?"

"It's new. Just showed up today."

Wenner's head snapped up and he looked joyful. Obviously this was somehow important or pleasing, but Corge had no idea how that could be. Sugar rock appeared and disappeared all the time.

Wenner was already on coms. "Send a team to Corge's bunk. Collect the sugar rock off his wall. Try not to break anything. He needs to continue to occupy the bunk."

The most frightening thing about that conversation to Corge was the fact that Wenner had to specify not to break stuff.

"Thank you so much, Corge. You've been a tremendous help," and that was the end of that. Wenner's face resumed its mask of concentration and Wenner turned to LeAnn.

"Resume your work in Vent Shaft 5 but com me if you see anything out of the ordinary, anything at all. Even if everything seems normal, have Corge file a deep report at the end of the project. Wait. Strike that. Have—what was your Apprentice's name?"

"Tracy," snapped LeAnn efficiently. She had a lot of Wenner in her.

"Right. Suresh's girl. Have Tracy do a data record on everything and then do a standard questionnaire routine on record afterward."

LeAnn nodded and they left. Vent shaft duty had gone from bad to worse. The duty itself bored Corge to tears. The prospect of filing a deep report would have been enough to ruin his night. But having to work with a full data record going *and then* having to answer a stupid autoquestionnaire might ruin his week depending on who decided to poke their noses into it.

As focused as she was, LeAnn felt the same way. She didn't say so outright, but her tone as she told Tracy to go collect the data record gear spoke volumes.

After Tracy ran off, LeAnn turned to Corge. "Let's get to work."

"Shouldn't we wait for the data record?"

LeAnn smirked. "What Wenner doesn't know, he can surmise. That's why he gets a high-quality food stipend."

CHAPTER 3

That night Corge didn't get back to his bunk until late. A big chunk of his wall had been removed, but the place was mostly clean. Thank goodness Wenner reminded the workers that Corge had to live there. In an odd way, Corge missed the sugar rock.

As he lay down on his bunk, he noticed that it wasn't entirely gone. Traces of it must have reached back into the wall, because he saw veins of the filmy substance deep in the hole they carved out.

He dragged his weary body up on his elbows, too interested not to investigate. Deep strands of the stuff traced along the edges of the hollow and looked like they met up and turned into big ropes that burrowed into the wall. If it was sugar rock, it must have grown through the rock.

Did they miss this, or was it something that formed since they left? He thought about waiting to report it in the morning, but a piece of him worried that if it was growing, it might hurt the integrity of his bunk. Granted, he was deep in the center of Armstrong, so the only thing on the other side should be more rock and then eventually a passageway corridor. But he certainly didn't want to lose air in his bunk to some oddball underground vacuum pocket.

A loss of air in his sleep could kill him, but more importantly, air was irreplaceable. In some future scenario, the dome might collapse and their society end just short of Earth's return because they were one bunkroom's worth of air short of what they needed.

Nobody wanted to be a "Schmitz Tripathi." The legendary System Ops Coordinator had left a valve unchecked on an exterior airlock. Nobody was killed, but it was estimated the failure leaked out enough air to lose the dome 10 years of operation considering the amount of time its recycling would compound usage. The dome was still estimated to be sustainable for 712 more years, but "pulling a Schmitz," or "Tripathi checking" had become serious insults. You always checked everything.

Corge dragged himself to the com and sent a message to Wenner. Surprisingly, Wenner was online and paying attention to incoming. He immediately shot back a note telling Corge he would be there with a team in 10 minutes.

Corge sighed. He knew his sleep clock would show a deficit and he'd be credited extra sleep time in the morning, but he wanted it now. He wanted it now so badly.

He had almost drifted off when Wenner and his three-member investigation team arrived. One of them was on Corge's competitive Go team. Though Corge had missed the last couple of matches, his teammate still gave him a cordial smile. The others apologized for interrupting his sleep. Wenner said, "When did you notice it?"

"As soon as I laid down," Corge sighed.

"Has it changed since you first saw it?"

Corge shook his head.

"Good. If you want, I can reassign you a bunk so you can get some sleep."

Corge was shocked at this. "Really?" he asked.

Wenner paused, which was very out of character. "I know I don't know the right things to say to make people feel at ease, but I do know what can be done. That's a thing that can be done and I can do it. Do you want me to do it?" He looked up at Corge with a hint of vulnerability.

Corge smiled. So Wenner was human. "Yeah, thanks Wenner. I'd love that. You're a friend."

Wenner stopped short at that. "Thanks, Corge. I'll order it now."

Corge found the temporary bunk and slept hard. His wake alarm went off at the normal time, meaning his profile had found the temp bunk too. It also meant he had to go to work. Which meant he had to find out where he was needed.

He had a message to report to Central, which made some sense given all the reports he had made. Probably some kind of debriefing. He pulled a breakfast tube out of the bunk's dispenser. He swore it tasted different, though theoretically all bunks dispensed the same protein mixture that simulated what eggs allegedly tasted like.

As Corge dragged himself out of the bunkroom, he found the corridor jumping with activity. People rushed by, which was somewhat unusual in Armstrong. The job of survival was mundane and boring. People knew pretty much what was expected of them at every moment. Rushing meant something was wrong.

He took off toward Central and experienced the odd sensation of jostling through a crowd. As he got near Central Control, the crowd thickened. Docking Bay was almost as full as a Disconnection Day ceremony. He actually had to squeeze his way to the stairs. He ran into LeAnn on the way. She looked annoyed by the crowd.

"You had no idea this was going on, did you? I tried to message you but the bunk said you were asleep."

"What is all this?" Corge asked.

"I'll tell you on the way. We're late."

As they fought through the crowd, LeAnn told Corge the situation in small bursts whenever they found some clear space. Ibrahima, the Communications Specialist, had called a closed session. Word got around that it was a direct result of a discovery made after finding out about Corge's sugar rock. Among other things, Ibrahima was charged with monitoring Earth. Any news involving her always set off a little extra interest.

"Also, you've been promoted," added LeAnn. "We have to check you in at the Generalists office on the way in. That's why I said we're running late."

Corge was speechless as LeAnn led him to the wing behind Central Control.

"Congratulations Corge," said Marina, head of Generalists assignments, herself a Generalist. She was also the mother of one of Corge's best friends as a student. It made him blush a little. "You're temporarily assigned to observation, off-world com and vent maintenance. These are acknowledged nonoptimals, Corge, so don't fret too much about the vent shaft one. I know you hate it," she smiled conspiratorially and touched his arm. "And I'm not supposed to tell you this, but it's marked for reassignment after whatever this current whosywhatzit is is over."

Corge just nodded, barely able to take it all in.

"Are we done?" LeAnn asked, barely restraining her impatience.

"Pretty much," answered Marina. "Just give me your Utility wrist and take this Generalist wrist and you're good to go. Everything else will update on its own— Oh! One more thing. Your bunk was declared a research site. Do you want a new one or are you fine in the temp for now?"

Corge said he was fine for now as he took off his old wrist module and put on the new Generalist one. He knew they wouldn't let him stay in the temp bunk for long, but he liked being close to Central.

LeAnn pulled him away but he stopped and turned back.

"Thanks Marina. I'm glad—I'm glad to see you today."

Marina smiled and said, "My pleasure, Corge. Now get along and do great things."

"What was that about?" LeAnn asked Corge as they raced upstairs to the Assembly Room.

"My mom and dad died in a redrill when I was 16. Marina sort of filled in as my mom for a few years."

That shut LeAnn up, which was why Corge rarely talked about it. He had come to terms with it and he didn't like making people feel bad about it.

Corge felt weird entering the Assembly Room after the meeting had already started, although he hadn't missed much. Ibrahima was on stage but the audience was still going through the "Iams," a rare formality.

To save long-term data storage capacity, not every meeting was recorded in full. When a meeting was important enough to record, it followed the formal rules. That meant starting with the Iams. In the early days, before Disconnection, each member of a meeting rose and stated, "I am from," and then named wherever they came from on Earth. It was a way of reaffirming their roots. Several generations later, every member was born in Armstrong. So as a reminder of their connection to the home planet, and to their hope of returning one day, members picked a place on pre-Disconnection Earth that one of their ancestors came from.

It quickly got around to LeAnn.

"I am from Pittsburgh."

That threw Corge off. He'd never heard LeAnn's Iam before. What was Pittsburgh? It wasn't one of the 31 Citadels of Earth. He wasn't even sure if it had been a museum city. He noticed LeAnn was staring at him and realized he was holding up the meeting.

"I am from Lagos."

LeAnn leaned over and whispered, "I'll tell you later."

The Iams finished and Ibrahima stood. She was tall for someone raised on Armstrong's diet and imposing with her bony brow and shining dark skin and hair. She seemed somehow to meet the gaze of everyone in the Assembly at once with her intense brown eyes.

"All of you know our history. But I want it fresh in our minds when I explain to you what we think happened with the tremor yesterday evening."

So it was a tremor, thought Corge. Not a disturbance or an explosion. A tremor.

"Right downstairs in the Control Center, we received our last transmission from Mexico City Citadel. That conversation is famous. It is re-enacted and reanalyzed every year on Disconnection Day.

"We all know how brave Colonel Jaime Ruiz informed the Armstrong Mission Control staff that Heretic crowds had torn down the infrastructure of the last Citadel. How Mexicontrol battled to stay in contact long after it fell.

"We know and mourn how, for more than a dozen orbits, Control Center staff tried to raise every one of the 31 Citadels and even some museum cities, with no success. And we know how the commanders of civilian and scientific missions called a joint address in Docking Bay, telling all the residents of the Armstrong Base that they would not be going home. That until Earth had worked out its troubles, everyone would need to pull together as one society and learn how to make Armstrong self-sufficient.

"What we'd like to forget and never should," Ibrahima intoned in the rhythm of a Disconnection Day speech, "what is important, especially on days like today, is to remember what happened next. I speak today not of the heroism that saved Armstrong. I speak of the chaos, of the suicides, of the abandonments. Because as shameful as we may feel they are, they were honest human responses, and they had consequences. We felt one of those consequences yesterday in the tremor."

Corge turned to LeAnn and raised an eyebrow. She raised one back.

"Yesterday we discovered the solution to two mysteries. The cause of both the tremor and the longstanding enigma of sugar rock were discovered in a long-abandoned and forgotten machine left on the plains south of Armstrong. But they raise another and deeper mystery, which will explain why I'm giving this address and not someone from History or Mechanics.

"Large traces of sugar rock were found in the bunkroom of Utility Worker Corge last night. Executive Wenner had been hoping to find a fresh report of sugar rock for some time. An excavation and examination of Corge's bunk walls showed ropes of white sugar-rock tendrils leading out of the station. That led to other and larger bundles of these ropes emanating from a point to the south.

"At that southern point, we found an egg-like device, about the size of a crate. Inside was a machine, the purpose of which is recorded in our database. But it had supposedly never been built. Apparently, it *had* been built, but whomever was working on it left us before it could be properly logged. Or possibly they deleted the record. Whatever the reason, it was not destroyed but abandoned on the Lunar plain where it sat, preserved for decades in a vacuum.

"Before Disconnection, as the Heretic threat rose, the Citadels created a plan to preserve all human knowledge against destruction, thus hoping to prevent another Dark Age. Two Citadel Preservation Modules were to be located on Earth and another one sent here. The amount of data was too great to transport wirelessly, so a system was built to receive it by rocket.

"The machine out there was constructed to receive and house the module. Its construction was kept secret due to concern that Heretical agents in Armstrong might try to prevent it from being installed. In any case, the data module never arrived. While we store and preserve much of the knowledge of pre-Disconnection Earth, the module would have been much more comprehensive and complete if it had.

"Now to the tremor. The machine out there was meant to preserve the data module against attack. Once the module was installed, a program was meant to go into action and re-form rock near the module into a long chain polymer that would be impenetrable without a key.

"That polymer is what we have been calling sugar rock. Somehow, within the past year or so, something activated the machine. It is either faulty or broken, and instead of creating the protective cocoon it was meant to, it has been sending malformed commands. As it used up rock nearby, it began to form the polymer in long strands that have shown up in Armstrong as sugar rock. The tremor itself was caused by falling rock in the crater walls, made unstable by the frequent attempts to form the polymer. The polymer itself is not dangerous and its creation poses no near-term threat to the dome's integrity. Nevertheless, long term, it could cause problems. A team is trying to shut it down or at least bring it under control.

"And now, the reason for this assembly. The Executives have decided to order a temporary team formed to investigate why the machine was reactivated. This might seem a frivolous exercise not related to the direct running and survival of Armstrong. In fact, those who favor the Passive approach to Reconnection believe that to be so. But the majority opinion is that even a moderate active Reconnection effort requires us to pursue this in case it leads to some kind of Earth communication."

The audience began to grumble. You rarely heard the word "Reconnection" spoken because so much rode on it. You didn't dangle that hope out there except as a distant aspiration. Ibrahima was treading dangerously close to the only thing that passed as heresy in Armstrong.

"I don't mean to be indelicate," she continued. "It is an infinitesimal chance. But think of the sugar rock. We deemed it irrelevant to investigate except as a hobby. However, when we were forced to look, it had deeper threads than we imagined, and that led us to a momentous discovery. For the record, I do not think that will happen in the case of the machine's reactivation. In fact, I'm almost certain we'll find it to be a bug or some errant transmission from Armstrong.

"But I am willing to countenance the idea that I might be wrong. And we have to remember that Reconnection is our prime objective. That is our ultimate survival goal. And we must prioritize its investigation appropriately.

LeAnn turned to Corge and whispered, "She must have barely won that decision or she wouldn't be spending so much time justifying it now."

Corge nodded.

Ibrahima spent the rest of the Assembly laying out the responsibilities of the team. Corge understood now why he received the Generalist assignments and why they were temporary. He was assigned to off-world com because they needed him on this new team. They probably wanted to boot him off as soon as it was done. On the other hand, Observation was a team he loved and excelled at and was part of this investigative team's core needs. He'd probably have the best chance of keeping that. He could stare at stars or rocks all day and find endless fascination there. People poked fun at the Observation team as the folks who "liked to watch paint dry." Corge sometimes felt himself wanting to argue that watching paint dry could be fascinating. He usually had the good sense to shut his mouth, though.

Finally, being put on the Vent Shaft team meant they wanted him to stay with LeAnn. It was why he got dragged into the whole mess in the first place. But he wasn't sure what more they could need from that part of the team. As the Assembly wound down, Ibrahima solved that mystery for Corge.

"LeAnn will lead the Vent Shaft teams in exploring and shoring up some older tunnels that lead out near the machine. If we're lucky, we may be able to move there and back almost entirely in pressure. There are reports of tunnels out there that aren't on the schematics. We'll have to see what shape they're in. It's a long shot but worth investigating."

As they adjourned, Corge felt lots of eyes on him. In a society as small and closed as Armstrong, that wasn't unusual. Everybody knew everyone else. But these weren't the normal looks and smiles. In an odd way, he was famous, or maybe notorious was a better word.

The feeling continued when he and LeAnn passed into the corridors. People looked at him with knowing expressions. People who usually ignored him made a point of nodding or saying hi.

"Get used to it," LeAnn said. "You're our latest star. Don't let it go to your head. Take 30 and meet me at Port 20. That's where we found the entry to the machine's secret passage. We're going to take a short investigative walk through it today."

Corge had to admit this sounded pretty exciting. If vent shaft work had always been like this, he might have been more enthusiastic. He smiled and nodded, "I'll try not to let the autographs take up all my break rest."

LeAnn snorted and moved off toward her own bunkroom.

CHAPTER 4

Chi-lin stood alone on the surface of the Moon, contemplating the machine that had scared the crap out of her when it shook the ground. She wanted revenge for that scare. Her boss laughed when she screeched during the tremor. Now, she was its master. Despite it being about three times her height, she had spent the last few hours repeatedly exploring every centimeter of its surface. She decided to examine the machine once more while she waited for the Vent Shaft team to arrive. She was the third Surface team member to go over the machine and so far found nothing new. She desperately wanted to find something new.

Chi-lin was an oddity in Armstrong. She hadn't been able to keep a job. Thankfully, there was no such thing as unemployment, but she kept being shuttled from assignment to assignment. Her Placement Executive found it puzzling and wasn't embarrassed to tell her so.

She had flown through the Student levels, whipped through Apprentice and Utility and seemed destined for stardom. Then she became a Generalist and everything fell apart. She always got commendations for some part of her job, even compliments on her brilliance. But then, somehow, she always let another part slip. In the Scheduling department, she received a commendation for her remastering of the main selection algorithm but eventually was reassigned because she kept forgetting to file her daily scheduling output.

"You can't be good at scheduling if you can't actually schedule people," her boss told her.

In Bio Development, she'd shown a particular talent for getting ferns to double biomass. Her supervisors had called it nothing short of magical. Everything else in her care died.

"If we could eat ferns exclusively, you'd never have to worry again," she'd been told. And then reassigned. All her assignments followed similar patterns.

So Chi-lin decided that she would break the pattern as a member of the Surface and Observation teams. So far she had been on time to all assignments, made no safety errors and, as far as she knew, had not missed any crucial observations.

These teams didn't require her to file weird reports, and she was in no danger of killing plants, so she figured the only thing that could torpedo her career here was missing an important observation. If she messed this up, she worried they might just give up on her and bust her down to Tender, and she'd spend the rest of her life emptying bins.

Despite her desire to collapse in a heap and sleep until the Tunnel team arrived, she went back over every inch of the machine. It was in shutdown mode, as far as they knew. The controls had been difficult to decipher. They were in an outdated pre-Disconnection dialect that used numbers as vowels, used names like "p0rt4lz" when it meant hatches and other such nonsense.

The Sociology department guessed it was a subculture language, most likely old when it was used and designed to confuse the Heretics. The Heretics weren't much on researching technology history since they hated technology. The Armstrong teams had some difficulty figuring it out themselves. The only way they found the power indicator was because one of the Surface team members was a science fiction fan. He guessed that the setting labeled "Roy" was a reference to a classic called *Blade Runner*. In that story, an artificial intelligence named Roy apparently had a famous line where he said, "Time to die." Didn't sound like that memorable of a line to Chi-lin but it turned out to be right. The "Roy" setting indicated how much time until the battery died.

Not that much, as it turned out. The machine still had power, likely collected from what stray photons hit it, but it was no longer humming like it had been when they found it.

Chi-lin felt her concentration drifting about halfway through the examination. She forced herself to refocus and noticed something she missed before. A small piece of material was wedged in one of the seams on the underside of the machine's main housing.

It looked like something got caught and torn off, so it likely wasn't hidden on purpose. She got out a flat tool and worked the thing out slowly and carefully. The seam was nonfunctional, but she wanted to make extra sure she didn't damage the machine or set off an alarm.

Nothing happened as she finally freed the wad of what looked like paper from inside the seam. Once she had it out, she wasn't sure how it had ever gotten in there. She began to think it had been stuck there on purpose. It looked like a piece of paper had been ripped off a larger sheet, folded up into a triangle and shoved into the seam. Perhaps whoever worked on the machine was approached by someone unexpected and didn't want it to be found.

She turned on her headcam recorder and noted the nature and placement of the find, then described the page as she unfolded it.

"Definitely paper. Looks like a printed page. There's a page number and some faded graphs. The consistency seems to be Disconnection Era printer book paper. One side is faded and damaged and doesn't seem to have much content. But look at the other side. Mama! That's, well you can read it, but that's a goddamned description of the whole project. They were in Salt Lake City! This was a coordinated effort."

She realized she was talking too much for documentation and wasting data space, so she stopped talking and made sure the paper was viewable in full from both sides for the recording.

Project Alexandria – Stage 3 – Lunar Receival

Polymer protection cocoons are capable, at both the Citadels and the remote launch station, of providing triple redundancy.

After copies are made at the SLC Museum Annex, one copy will be entangled to the New York Citadel and a physical copy will be launched to Citadel 32 at Armstrong.

While this attempt provides for local remote physical and remote virtual copies, it is quite possible that not all copies will be successful. In view of this risk, all Archive houses will be constructed to act as a final and sole repository, if necessary.

Unlock keys are detailed on page 34 but will exist in series with a private destructible key on site and a public remote key in series. Thus, the SLC key will also be stored in New York, the New York key in Citadel 32 and the Citadel 32 key in the SLC Museum Annex.

These keys are considered uncrackable and the polymer protection is considered unbreakable. While advances may supersede these statements, the current state of the Heretical Uprising indicates advancements are unlikely, should conditions prevail that require protections.

Thus the system is evaluated as 98.7% secure. While not normally within this Construction's tolerances, given conditions on the ground, it will serve.

All stations must be kept entirely clandestine. While Citadel 32 is remote, it is highly probable that Heresy Agents are embedded in Armstrong Staff. Therefore, Citadel 32 is no exception to strict confidentiality rules.

It is entirely preferable for the Archive mechanism to become permanently locked than for the key to fall into the wrong hands. If hostile agents do attain the private key, they will attempt to activate and destroy the Archive.

CHAPTER 5

An alert told Chi-lin that the team had arrived at the tunnel hatch. She went over and began system checks to help them out of the hatch and onto the surface. Amid the routine safety communications, they all squawked about the paper Chi-lin had found.

"Does it look weathered, or is it fresh?" one of the team asked.

"Faded on one side, but on the other, so fresh, it could have just been printed. No sun damage or weathering, just the fold marks and of course the tear where it was ripped," Chi-lin answered.

"Any smudges or fingerprints or notations or anything?"

Chi-lin realized she hadn't actually looked, so she stopped when she got a chance and examined the paper again. She had carefully set it on the ground away from where she was working. No air meant no wind, meaning it was the safest place she could think of to keep it while she worked on the hatch.

"There's one small smudge. Can't tell what it might be. Otherwise, no other markings," she finally reported then set the page back down.

They speculated excitedly about what it could mean, particularly the references to SLC and New York, then settled down as they got close to opening the hatch.

The Surface teams had explored the tunnel from both ends, but this would be the first time anyone had actually used it to come out to the surface. The airlock that existed in the tunnel had needed a lot of work. It was operable but not at the tolerances Armstrong had developed over the years of its survival. Back when the lock had been built, it was fine to let some gas vent into the atmosphere. These days, Armstrong attempted to save every molecule.

Everything looked right and all the gas had been vented back into the interior tunnel. Chi-lin gave the team the green signal to open the hatch from their side. The airlock worked well, but even so, a small puff of gentle wind came along when the hatch opened.

"We'll definitely have to fix that," one of the team said.

With horror, Chi-lin turned and saw the gentle puff of wind had blown the piece of paper what seemed like several kilometers. With no air resistance to slow it, it was still going.

"Shit!" she yelled and took off after it.

It kept moving in a straight line, and worse, slowly rising. Chi-lin wasn't sure what the escape velocity of a piece of paper was, but she didn't want to find out.

As she got close, she could see it was just starting to get out of her reach. She had to be careful. If she jumped too hard, she might shoot right past it and end up landing far away. But she was going to have to jump. She let instinct take over and executed an elegant pirouette, snagged the piece of paper gently, careful not crumple it, and landed only a few feet away.

While she couldn't hear it, she could see the Tunnel team was giving her a round of applause. She took a bow and began jumping back toward them, tripping on a dark rock she thought had been a shadow and almost launching herself back at high velocity.

When she got back to the group, one of the Archivists said, "You know, you already scanned the info from that. My guess is they'll probably recycle it. We could use the carbon."

Chi-lin just stared through her visor while another teammate said, "Oh, leave her alone, Ahira. She deserves to keep the page for finding it as well as for that graceful retrieval."

Her earpiece became a riot of static as everyone laughed at once, stepping on one another.

As the laughter died down, a man asked, "May I see it?"

It was Corge. Chi-lin definitely recognized Armstrong's poster boy from the recordings that had been made available of his sugar rock discovery and his appearance at the Assembly.

He held his hand out but slowly lowered it and looked rejected as if she might refuse.

"Oh, sorry," she recovered. "Here."

Corge stared at the page, front and back, for a few minutes before Specialist LeAnn interrupted.

"He may be like that for a while. It's part of his job as an Observation team member. He's just getting used to being allowed to stare at things. Show us the machine. He'll catch up."

Chi-lin showed the Tunnel team over to the white egg-shaped machine. They would take measurements and observations of their own, but she delivered a good overview to limit the duplication of work.

The structure had been designed to look like a flower with a wide opening at the top, accessed by several panels that folded out. The lower part was made of similar curved panels fitted together with minimal seams, one of which was where Chi-lin found the wad of paper.

The most interesting observations would likely be made from the top. A series of transmission boxes and antennas were attached to the inside of the curved metal panels. They looked as if they would have collapsed against each other to make a powerful internal broadcast system untouchable from the outside.

A ring of machines set around the inside of the egg just under the panel hinges had hummed when the machine was first found. Tubes ran up from this ring in several places. At the ends of the tubes, hundreds of tiny filaments spread out. The best guess was that these created the polymer generation field. The surface around the machine was covered with examples of sugar rock, some of which had built up along the base of the egg and towered up along its side. One of these towers had grown hundreds of meters high with a base approximately 10 meters thick. This one had partially collapsed, causing the tremors. The system had been meant only to create a coating of polymer several centimeters thick on the outside of the egg to protect it from unauthorized use. It had gone seriously wrong.

"The antenna system is also meant to be the key lock," said Corge who had quietly rejoined the group. Everyone stopped looking at the giant tower of sugar rock and back at the top of the egg. "I'm pretty sure that's what the diagram on the back is showing. See?"

He pointed back and forth between the hinged opening at the top of the egg and the drawing. Suddenly, everyone could see that the random-looking drawing actually depicted a series of flaps and antennas with dotted lines indicating movement paths and a final state.

"This is the unified antenna that would allow it limited communication from inside the metal plates and the sealing polymer, our sugar rock. But you see this one filament. We'll have to investigate it, but from the diagram it looks like it is a dedicated line connecting directly to the locking mechanism of the plates and the ring system for generating the polymer."

"But how does the rock get unlocked once it's sealed?" asked LeAnn.

"The same way sugar rock disappears, I guess?" Corge answered. "I'm only guessing now, but I assume the reason sugar rock appears and disappears is because it's signal dependent somehow. The faulty machine was sending creation and dissolution signals intermittently."

Nobody said anything. Corge realized it must be a ridiculous idea. "I mean that's pretty far-fetched, I admit. It's probably something else, but—"

"No," said Ahira, the woman who had been teasing Chi-lin earlier. "That makes sense. We've been trying to replicate that. We have some records of Earth tech that could wirelessly convert rock to other materials with targeted resonance waves. I'm guessing that's what this was, tuned specifically to Lunar materials. Once you can convert it one way, it seems like it's dead simple to turn it the other. We just were too stupid to do it ourselves."

Chi-lin finished the machine demo by showing off the inside, but the fun part was over. All the gear was in the top. When you climbed inside, all you found were support struts and ports meant to accommodate other parts.

"I wish we had a diagram of the Archive box that was supposed to fit in here," sighed Sharif, a Generalist on the History and Earth Com teams. "We can derive a lot from the shape of the space here, but I'd love to see how it was supposed to interact with the capsule."

"We're certain the box never arrived?" asked Corge, staring out across the landscape.

"Well, it's not here," pointed out LeAnn.

"What's that?" he pointed out in the direction Chi-lin had come from after chasing down the paper.

"What?" Everyone looked. "There's nothing there," said LeAnn.

"No, there is," said Chi-lin, catching eyes with Corge. "You mean the thing I tripped on."

"The what?" asked Corge. "I don't know, but I see a low, black box out there. Did you trip on it?"

"I thought it was a shadow at first. But then I tripped on it and was too worried about the paper at the time to pay any attention to it.

Within a few minutes, everyone was trudging out toward the low, flat shadow Corge had pointed out. Most of them still couldn't really make it out.

It turned out to be a flat metal box covered with solar panels and was very definitely receiving a signal of some sort.

"It looks like a repeater," said Sharif.

"What's a repeater?" asked LeAnn.

Chi-lin piped up a little too eagerly. "It's old Earth tech for signal boosting. They used it a lot in the last days before Disconnection to communicate with Armstrong. It takes a weak signal and reamplifies it to pass it along. There are three of them in Central Control still. They're always left on in low power mode to—"

"All right, Chi-lin. We can see how smart you are," snapped Ahira. "What's it doing out here? This one ours? Another lost one?"

"I doubt it," said Sharif. "Chi-lin's right though," he gave her a sympathetic look. "This is a repeater and there's really only one reason to have one. It must have been placed out here a long time ago to amplify signals to the machine. And it looks like it's getting a signal."

"From where?" asked LeAnn.

"Earth," said Corge.

CAPITULUM 1

Michael always worried that his candle would sputter out before he got to the Reliquary. He couldn't check out a volt-light like most visitors. He had to use a candle or Superior Dabashi would know about the trips and would ask questions, and then Michael wouldn't be able to carry out his secret project.

But the candle never actually went out. His walking was the only thing that caused a breeze in the dark halls. The ruined tower that housed the Reliquary was a silent and lonely place, which was why he liked it. In fact, that was why he first began coming to the Reliquary. He wanted to be alone in a place of great sacredness in case anyone found him. He could say he was meditating. It just happened to also be a place deep within the lonely remains of the Citadel, which was rumored to be occupied by ghosts or Heretics, or both. So it was sparsely populated, to say the least. Superior Guteerez was the only official assigned to the place.

One room in the Reliquary in particular fascinated Michael. It's where he spent all his time these days. It was an empty room on the first floor far from Guteerez's chambers. Inside sat a white object about twice as tall as Michael. From what he could tell, it was some sort of a machine from before the Fall. That was the real reason he continued to come back. He wanted to figure out how it worked, what its purpose was. He couldn't fathom its power source or its function, but he kept discovering new things about it.

When he first visited the room, he took it for a sculpture. As he sat and meditated that day, he noticed wires. He discovered a box connected to it that had a battery and showed some kind of unintelligible moving text. Eventually, he figured out how to make a small, thin piece of metal rise and fall from the top. A toy? A moving work of ancient Citadelian sculpture? Possibly. But to Michael, it seemed too complex, or maybe complex in the wrong ways, to simply be a piece of art.

The main body of the piece was some kind of semitransparent rock. It seemed there was metal below its surface, but the clear rock was impenetrable. Who knew what ancient power had embedded the metal in the rock or where the odd rock had come from? The piece was egg-shaped, and a thin piece of metal rose out of an impossibly tiny hole in the top.

He knew it could do more. He just needed more time. To have more time, he needed to make sure nobody, especially Dabashi, found out he came here. And to that end, he needed to bring candles. If he requested volt-lights, they would want to know what he was using them for. Candles were free.

Today, he decided to go over every inch of the Sculpture, looking for anything he might have missed. He hoped to find a lever or a compartment or something that would allow him to look inside. He knew some old Citadelian things had hatches for workmen to repair them. Even some statues had hollowed-out internals, like the huge copper lady that lay in the water to the south.

He meticulously moved his hands over the surface. He kept moving his candle to make sure he could see where his hands were going. The surface felt smooth and cool, as usual. He thought about the person who built it. What noble artisan of the Citadel of New York had wrought it? Was he proud? Was he famous? Or maybe he was a Middler like Michael, someone born into a good enough family to do good works but almost never allowed to rise into the inner circles of the Authority.

He marveled at how irregular the surface was. It was probably not intentional. Or was it part of the artistic expression? Was it a comment on the unpredictable nature of our world? He doubted it. That was the way the Heretics thought, not the Citadelians. The Heretics rebelled against the Citadels because there was not enough unpredictability. They complained about overplanning and stagnation and then brought the world into chaos.

Citadelian artists surprised him sometimes with their freedom of expression. It was one of the most confusing aspects of history. The Citadels allowed great freedoms. Many more freedoms than people had under the Authority. The Superiors taught that as the lesson of the Fall. It was too much freedom. Humanity could not handle it. The confusing part for Michael was that the Heretics rebelled on the basis of too much control. Yet they had ultimate freedom. Why didn't they just go off to a museum city and live however they wanted?

Michael never risked expressing his thoughts on the matter, but he felt there must not have been the right kind of freedom or the Heretics wouldn't have rebelled. The thing that troubled him most was that the failings of the Citadels seemed to confirm the Heretics' view. And yet the Authority praised the Citadels and preserved their traditions while purging the Heretics, hunting them to extinction.

Of course he had nobody to ask. To question the basis of the Authority out loud would be heresy and grounds for expulsion, imprisonment or worse. That's why he loved to hide in the Reliquary. He could grapple with those questions in the silent presence of the remnants of the Citadel without fear for his life. The worst that could happen would be someone might discover him and tell him he really should inform his Superiors when he meditated there. It wasn't wrong to go to the Reliquary as a Monk, after all. It was only a slight oversight not to let anyone know he went there.

Michael thought it would ruin everything if the Superiors knew he was there. He wasn't sure exactly why. His direct Superior, Dabashi, was kind for the most part. Not very warm but always fair. However, when it came to the Citadel ruins, Dabashi got prickly and very argumentative. He never transgressed propriety, just always made it harder to justify activities in the Citadel than other things. It was as if he was trying to reduce the number of people who went there and the amounts of time those who did spent there.

Michael's fingers caught on something. He had stopped paying attention to what he was doing but his fingers had continued to methodically feel over every square inch of the egg. Down near the bottom, in deep shadow, where he might not have been brave enough to touch if he'd been looking, he found something.

It felt like a small bit of paper rolled up. He got his candle as near to the edge as he could but could not shed enough light into the crevice to see what he was doing. At least he could tell there were no spiders. He wasn't sure if it was wedged under the Sculpture or embedded in it or—then he felt it move.

It was wedged in a ripple in the flowing bumpy surface. Someone had tucked it into a small gap between two of the larger bumps. He tried to pull it out, but it wouldn't budge. But he felt it move, so he was sure he could move it more. He kept working at it until his candle went out.

Michael slumped down against the egg, giving up for the moment. He had another candle to light off the first but he had nothing else with which to make flame. He knew the room had a tinderbox somewhere, but he was wedged deep behind the Sculpture with his arms almost caught below it. If he got up now to look for the tinderbox, he wasn't sure he could find the paper again. He sighed and decided to keep trying. The candlelight hadn't helped him much anyway.

Suddenly the dim glow of a volt-light bathed the room. Michael heard voices. Someone was coming. He scrunched up his legs so they weren't visible and squeezed himself into a hiding place behind the Sculpture without letting go of the paper. He could tell one of the voices was Superior Dabashi. The light brightened and the owners of the voices entered the chamber Michael was in.

"I told you he wasn't here," said Guteerez, the Citadel Reliquary's Warden. Michael always made sure to slip in without Guteerez noticing. It was easy enough to come from the attached Monastery, which didn't require a security gate like the other entrances.

"And *I* know he does come here and too often," said Dabashi. "He's likely to break something."

"Break something?" asked the elder Guteerez. "You talk as if he's a child. What could he break? The Archive is empty anyway."

"Quiet! Don't call it that in public."

"I wasn't aware we were in public," Guteerez laughed. "Look, Dabashi. I know your charge. And thankfully, I don't know your secrets, and maybe that's why I worry less. But this old rock here isn't going anywhere for anyone. There's nothing in it to find—that much I do know. At worst, he discovers how to deploy the antenna. He won't even know what it is and it certainly won't work for him. He'll think it's a moving sculpture, and that's pretty much what it is."

"And if he finds out that much, he becomes dangerous. We ought to lock off this chamber," snapped Dabashi.

"And make it even more attractive? No. If he's coming here as often as you say, and I am surprised I don't see him, he must be quite stealthy. But if he comes here that often, he's probably going through the questioning phase we all went through at his age. He needs his quiet time. Eventually, he'll stumble across his own answers. If we push him, we risk driving him away—or worse. Let him stew. Let him sit. Let him write angry young poetry if he must. But calm down. He won't find what you fear. It isn't here to be found."

"It makes me nervous." Dabashi paused, muttering. "But perhaps you're right. If that's the case, maybe we should lean the other way.

I'll approach him. Tell him I know he's been coming here and that I'll countenance it. Make it part of his rituals to come contemplate here. That way I'll know when he's coming."

"That's an excellent idea." Michael could hear Guteerez grinning. "Smart. Make it a chore! Take the mystery out of it! He'll tire of it in half the time."

"Very well. Take him to luncheon and make the assignment tomorrow. Make it a commission. But mind you, I want him checking in with you. No more sneaking in through the side halls."

"Very good. Now let's go before we miss evening ale."

Michael was so stunned he almost let go of the paper. The two Superiors walked away, plunging the room into darkness. He had doubled his knowledge of the Sculpture, fired his desire to uncover its mystery and come to understand he would be given sanction to spend every day in the room, all for the price of checking in with Guteerez.

Then another thought struck him. Dabashi would know when Michael was there and likely try to observe him—quite a heavy extra price to pay but just about worth it. He wasn't sure what Dabashi could do. Stop him from looking at the Sculpture? Stop him from observing the battery box? Stop him from—the paper came loose.

Somehow he had wiggled it the right way or loosened it up enough that it slid out from between the two bumps in the surface. He pulled it away and discovered it was a rolled up page of paper. He unrolled it but couldn't see a thing. He desperately wanted to see what it said but he had no light.

He scrambled around in the dark with one hand gently holding the paper while he used his other hand to search for the tinderbox. He finally found it. He had to trust the paper to lay on a chair without disappearing while he worked the tinder blindly on his spare candle. Eventually, he lit it. The paper had not disappeared.

On the page was an unintelligible drawing. It looked like a diagram. One of the shapes seemed vaguely like the Sculpture, but much smoother and with its top lopped off. There were all kinds of squiggles and dotted lines and words in a language Michael couldn't read.

On the other side was a page of text titled "Signal Transmission Instructions." This was in a variant of English that was ancient but Michael had studied enough Citadelian texts to be able to read most of it.

SIGNAL TRANSMISSION INSTRUCTIONS

The following instructions apply to the NYC module and Archive Beta.

As a reminder, the primary Archive is located in the SLC part of the Ellay Citadel (LAC). The location of SLC is classed.

The NYC module exists as a local connected backup, and the Armstrong Archive (ALC) will serve as a physical remote backup.

NYC will be entangled with LAC, impacting direct communication between the two. An explanation of the entanglement preservation envelope and the associated effects (translated experiences) can be found under the section "Entanglement Protocol Advisories."

For the purposes of this section, no communication attempts should be made from the NYC module to the SLC module.

All transmissions should be forwarded through ALC whether meant for ALC or SLC. The following steps should be taken to engage transmission.

BEGIN AUTHORIZATION

Set the control box to a dedicated wavelength. Use a Dabashi key to attune the wavelength to your authorized frequency. Temporary Dabashi keys may be provided by an authorized party to grant limited transmission permissions to a second operator. Follow normal two-person presence auth schemes at the control box.

Once granted auth, the operator will see several transmission selections, defaulted to a single stream simpledata message. More complex messages may be accommodated by adjusting these settings. Consult the section "Archive Messaging Settings." Since the transmissions are meant mostly for maintenance and status, assume all settings are left as default.

BEGIN MESSAGE CREATION

Select "Generate" to move to the message creation selection.

Message Creation consists of two parts. The first part is for transmission header and codeword protocols, the identification needs of the message. The second part is for the message content.

Identification needs should follow standard procedure as coordinated by the Archive Central Project. In absence of updated procedures, as in a failure of one module or an emergency situation, use the most recent emergency control procedures to create an identity.

IMPORTANT: Failure to enter an acceptable identification section will result in lockout, despite authorization.

Message content is freeform but will be analyzed at recipient end for steg signals as required in training.

Once identification scheme is validated and content has been entered to the satisfaction of the user, select Transmission Bundling to move to Transmission Selection.

BEGIN TRANSMISSION

Once in Transmission Selection, make sure the transmitter is deployed as described in the section "Antenna Control and Deployment."

If the antenna is deployed, whether the Archive is in closed or open state, the operator should be able to make visual confirmation. Once this confirmation is made, select Transmission and provide confirmation.

Progbars will indicate transmission operation. Once the progbar is complete, it will slide and a receiptbar will display. Once automatic receipt is indicated, the receiptbar will fill and visually indicate estimated message coherence.

Once the receiptbar is complete, the receiving module may ask for cross-ver. Use current or emergency protocols to provide response in these cases. While this will not affect transmission itself, it may affect the end module's ability or willingness to respond.

Please keep in mind that while the Earth-Lunar message transit is only a few seconds, the processing of encryption, decryption and verification take several times that amount.

SUMMARY

Sending maintenance and status messages over the Archive should not be used to replace normal comm means. However some sensitive communications will be necessary and direct module-to-module comm is preferable in these situations. For that reason, module transmission has been made as simple and secure as possible.

See this link (or reverse in print) for illustration aids.

Michael had no idea what most of the words on the page meant. Well, that wasn't exactly true. Michael knew most of the words, it was the sentences he couldn't make much sense of. The one word that leaped out at him was "Dabashi."

"Use a Dabashi key to attune the wavelength to your authorized frequency. Temporary Dabashi keys may be provided by an authorized party to grant limited transmission permissions to a second operator."

While Michael wasn't completely sure, he guessed this meant that there was a key named after Dabashi that made the control box work and further, a person with that key could unlock the control box for a second person to use.

What Michael dared to hope was that the Dabashi key might be genetic. He had heard of that sort of thing before. If it was, and Superior Dabashi had the right genes, he could be tricked into unlocking the control box in a way that would let Michael use it. Michael had no idea how he would orchestrate that without Dabashi suspecting what was going on. Of course, he could also be wrong about the key. In which case, getting caught might be even worse.

Dabashi had promised to keep an eye on Michael. So getting Dabashi in the room should be easy. Michael was also fairly confident he could play around enough with the control box to know what state it needed to be in to accept an unlock.

The real trick, if the control center activated whatever it was supposed to activate, would be to get Dabashi to leave without shutting Michael down, reporting him, or getting him declared a Heretic. Michael wasn't sure anything he planned to do was technically heretical, but he'd seen the accusation used as a weapon too often to believe a reason was really needed. Once you were accused of being a Heretic, your life was miserable even if you were one of the rare people who escaped conviction. The only exceptions were state-appointed opposition Heretics, sort of devil's advocates. Michael knew he didn't have the constitution to make a career of pretending to be a Heretic under state supervision. He wouldn't lurk about playing with ancient Citadelian relics if he did.

Michael thought back over the conversation between Dabashi and Guteerez, and the makings of a plan formed.

CHAPTER 6

"Do the words change the longer you look at them?"

LeAnn sat down next to Corge, holding a cup of coffee, smiling.

"I wish they did. I feel like I've squeezed every last drop of meaning from it, but something's still nagging me. Something's still missing."

The paper from the machine sat on the café table in front of Corge. He eyed LeAnn's coffee suspiciously.

"Don't worry. I'll be careful," she said. "I can't believe they let you carry that thing around, anyway."

"They don't care," Corge replied. "It's scanned. If anything, they'd like an excuse to reclaim it now that we have the info. I suppose I'm being a little sentimental wanting to keep it, but somehow I feel like the digital version wouldn't be as easy to decipher. Except that I seem to be having plenty of trouble deciphering it as it is."

LeAnn took a sip of the coffee and looked at Corge over the rim of the cup, "Good thing you're assigned to Observation. If you were just on my Tunnel team I'd tell you to quit navel-gazing and get back to work," she grinned.

That was the joke about Observation team members, especially Generalists who were on more than one team. When they wanted to slack off, they insisted they were studying something, like a speck of dirt, or a hole in the wall, or a piece of paper. Corge looked up and caught LeAnn's grin.

"Stop it," he said.

"What?" she looked genuinely surprised. "Can't a former team supervisor smile at the most famous man in Armstrong? Or are you past enjoying that sort of thing now that you're Mr. Famous Famousman from Famous Dome on the Moon of Famous."

That frightened Corge. Was she flirting?

He started to say something and she interrupted.

"I'm only teasing you, Corge. But you are famous, so you better be able to deal with it when someone who means it starts messing with you. If you know what I mean."

She got up with her coffee and walked out of the café. Was she strutting? Corge wasn't sure what she meant or whether he was imagining things she might have meant. His mind was still too sunk in the paper to spend much time trying to figure it out.

It was titled "Lunar Receival" but it was all about security. Public keys most likely referred to an encryption system. He'd spent some time with the Data Systems team getting briefed. Visions of Bob and Alice attacking each other with keys still filled his head with confusion, but he thought he understood the basics enough to know what the paper meant. What nagged at him were the keys being stored in series.

SLC was most likely Salt Lake City, a small museum city that had been located in mid-east Ellay, or somewhere near there. One of the data analysts suggested they were mimicking one of the standard data backup protocols, with a local virtual backup being SLC and a physical backup being Armstrong.

If that was the case, though, why give the public key for New York to the Moon? The public key allows you to decrypt a message from the holder of the private key. So if Armstrong had the New York key, it was meant to receive messages from New York and could only send messages to SLC. But if NYC was the primary, that seemed backward.

It wasn't.

"It's not the primary. SLC is," said Corge, standing up. I think I know what happened."

Several people looked at him. Some smiling. A pretty young Generalist about Corge's age asked what everyone else was thinking. "What happened, Corge?"

"They backed it up in New York. We need to try to target a message to New York."

This quieted the crowd. Talk of messaging Earth in any way was considered borderline psychotic except in very serious conversations. Shouting an outburst in the middle of the café in Armstrong, even if you were Corge, was in poor taste.

Corge didn't care. He flew out of the café, clutching the paper tightly.

CAPITULUM 2

When the messenger arrived inviting Michael to luncheon with Guteerez, he tried to act suitably surprised. He felt pressure enough keeping up the act until Guteerez revealed the reason for the meal. Then he realized he also had to get Guteerez to help him trick Dabashi into unlocking the control box. Which meant more half-lying.

"Thank you," was all he could mutter to the messenger, who didn't seem to notice Michael's inner turmoil and left.

The luncheon was in the Superior's garden in a building diagonal from the Citadel ruins. Michael was expected, so he had the disconcerting experience of being able to walk right into the garden without anyone asking him what he needed.

He wondered how they knew. He hadn't been asked to the garden more than twice, but they always knew. The community was small enough that they might know him by sight, though he certainly didn't know all of them.

As respectful as the staff was of his right to be there, they still completely ignored him. It would not do to be caught unable to assist a Superior because they were wasting time speaking with a Monk.

Michael found Superior Guteerez at a table near a corner overlooking the street below. Guteerez waved and motioned for Michael to take a seat.

"Thank you for joining me here, Michael. I know it may seem ominous, but I do so love the garden and I felt maybe you would enjoy sitting with me today. Of course, someday I'm sure you will be able to avail yourself of it whenever you want."

This sort of condescending pleasantry was typical of the Superiors—apologizing for their position while rubbing it in your face at the same time.

"But I promise this meeting will all be to the good. In fact, you should be pleased, I expect."

"Thank you, Superior."

As Michael expected, there was a long, polite meal of small talk with Guteerez trying to tease out Michael's opinion on several of the other Superiors. Michael did not realize Guteerez was such a gossipmonger.

Guteerez brought up the Citadel, which they could see from their seats. Michael knew where the conversation was going. He spoke up so he wouldn't just sit there trying not to look suspicious and asked what Guteerez thought of the legendary 32nd Citadel.

"The supposed Citadel on the Moon?" Said Guteerez between bites. He grunted. "It's an intriguing possibility. I'm suspicious only of my own desire to want it to be true. How marvelous would it be to know that the civilization of the Citadelians survived untouched, secured by the vacuous space above us, which the Heretics could never cross. "It is a fine, fine thought, my boy, yes it is. But sadly all too unlikely."

"Why is that?" Michael asked, noting Guteerez hadn't denied the 32nd Citadel's existence, as many Superiors did. The church itself did not rule on the matter, deeming it open for speculation. Anything deemed open for speculation was essentially irrelevant and not worth serious time. That made it a perfect topic for idle conversation over a luncheon in the Superior's garden.

"Don't get me wrong, Michael. I don't disbelieve there was a settlement on the Moon. It was called Armstrong by all accounts. And I know it was often referred to as a Citadel, but even the 'Delians' own texts indicate it was a ceremonial title.

"No, my young man, it was a settlement. Not even as grand as a museum city like Hartford or Boston. It's the physics of it that douse my fires of belief in the end.

"Let's say that Armstrong was a thriving settlement full of scientists and leaders, much like our own. It would need to be constrained. By all accounts, there is no atmosphere on the Moon. They would have to build an airtight structure in which to live and move all the materials to build it up to the Moon. That right there argues against their survival.

"If one simple leak springs, they would all suffocate as the air escaped. And they have no source of new materials to fix it. Before the Fall, they could have called for a ship from Earth, but not anymore, you see. But let's say they don't spring a leak. What would they eat? There are no more foods coming from us, and according to the ancients, the Moon's soil is not fertile. Even if they could grow foods inside their structure, we already said it must be space constrained. They wouldn't have enough room to grow enough food to feed themselves.

"But even setting that aside," Guteerez warmed to the topic now, waving his hands and then wiping his mouth with a napkin. "Hmm. Maybe they discover some amazing new way to grow food in a vacuum among the Moon rocks. Yes? Fine. But think of all the other resources they don't have. What about medicine? A flu could wipe them all out in a snap," he clicked his fingers. "There can be no real law enforcement. There was no need of it when the population turned over regularly. But keep them confined and it's not unlikely they go 'lunatic.' The word does derive from their adopted home, and they have no police force to stop the killing!

"No, I'm afraid there are just too many perils for a settlement like that to have survived. Perhaps one day we will rediscover the secrets of the ancients and cross that black expanse. Then we may find the ruins of the 32nd Citadel, so-called, and in their records regain a bit of our own history. But not soon, I'm afraid. No, not soon."

This depressed Michael more than he had expected.

"But you look so down now? Here I am putting us off our digestion with macabre tales of disaster. I apologize. Let me cheer you up with the reason I've met with you today."

"Of course, Superior, but first a question, if I may?"

Guteerez seemed surprised at this but nodded for Michael to go ahead.

"I only look disappointed because you are most likely right. And I, like you, long for that dream to be true. To have some piece of our past that isn't ruined or spoiled by the Heretics. I've often wondered if it were possible to send a message to the Moon."

Guteerez started to look impatient.

"But my question. Even if you are right that they have not survived, which you most likely are, could there still be machines running that could answer us? Perhaps powered by the sun as some of the rarest 'Delian relics are? Could they have left something here that has gone unrecognized and thus survived through the Fall safely, giving us the key?"

Guteerez's smile went from impatient to generous.

"Just so, my boy, just so. It's unlikely, but we can't be sure until we've looked for it, eh? Which brings me to the reason for this delightful luncheon beyond its inherent pleasures, which have not been few. Now, I know you spend quite a bit of time in the Reliquary with the Scuplture. No, no, it's quite all right," Guteerez held up a hand to stop a protest, which Michael hadn't been mounting. So he belatedly started to mount one. "I would prefer you didn't sneak behind my desk, but that's past, and no rules were broken in any case."

Michael tried to think what look he should be giving right then, which left him with a sort of befuddled expression that unintentionally suited the moment quite nicely.

"Dabashi asked me to formalize your investigation of the Sculpture—commission you, actually. You are to spend at least an hour a day—more if it doesn't conflict with other responsibilities—communing in the Reliquary and examining the Sculpture. This will be part of your rituals now. So you'll need to check in with me, and you'll need to answer inquisition when necessary on the matter."

Michael found it wasn't that hard to make himself smile with anticipation. "Thank you, Superior. Of course. This is most gratifying."

"Think nothing of it, boy. Just let it be a lesson that you don't need to sneak around to get what you want. It only raises suspicions. Go through channels," here the Superior wagged his finger. "You'll find it's not as intimidating or unforgiving as you might think." Guteerez chuckled as if he had made a particularly funny joke.

Michael didn't see the humor, knowing plenty of colleagues who went through channels and got censured or worse. But he laughed along with Guteerez anyway.

When the laughter died down, Michael took the plunge.

"I wonder if I might be so bold as to presume upon your generosity with aid and assistance?" He didn't say it exactly like a Formal Request for Aid, but figured mixing in some of the phrasing might make him seem respectful and hide his nervousness.

"My, my. Almost a Formal Request for Aid, that was. What could be so important?" Guteerez's smile turned just a touch fatherly and another touch mocking.

"Superior Dabashi is not fond of me, but I believe he could be very helpful in my examination of the Sculpture." An unexpected look of jealousy crossed Guteerez's face. Michael wondered if the Superior was aware of it. "Obviously, I will need your constant guidance and aid as well, but that is, if you'll pardon my clumsy phrasing, well that's why you hold the Office of the Citadel. I have no doubt I will rely on you much."

The jealous look softened but didn't totally leave. Michael forged on.

"Superior Dabashi does not share your interest or enthusiasm. Even so, he is good with mechanics."

"Is something in the Sculpture of a mechanical nature?" Guteerez raised an eyebrow.

Michael had to make a decision. Did he hold back the facts and lose a chance to get Dabashi involved? Or did he reveal the moving filament and risk bringing undue attention? He made his decision.

"I have discovered a control box that causes a filament to come up out of the Sculpture and then come down again. I'm not sure what its—"

"It's an antenna," Guteerez chuckled, though not quite so pleasantly. "The Sculpture could have had many reasons for sending or receiving information. It may have incorporated adaptations of some sort for special occasions, or it may have merely kept track of who saw it. Many of these old relics had similar functions, seemingly wasteful to our sensibilities, but the Citadelians were wealthy and powerful beyond imagining."

"You think Superior Dabashi would not be interested?"

"Oh, he'll be quite interested," Guteerez smirked.

"Perhaps too interested?" ventured Michael.

Guteerez looked like he'd swallowed something unexpected. "Well, not to speak ill of a fellow Superior, of course. But I suspect when you have been avoiding me, you just might also have been avoiding the Superior's interest, maybe?"

The look Guteerez gave Michael had an odd mix of understanding and fear with a slight touch of anger. Michael had never seen such a look before from anyone, definitely not from a Superior. It almost made him feel Guteerez was on his side. Almost.

"I welcome the Superior's interest always, of course," replied Michael carefully. "But—" he wasn't sure how to put it.

"But sometimes you need the space to make mistakes as a young man," Guteerez finished, smiling. "And one of our Superior's best traits is his famous lack of tolerance for faults." He said this last almost to himself.

"Just so. Superior, this is my request. How can I get the benefit of his expertise while still being able to, uh, make my mistakes?"

"Of course," Guteerez looked almost gleeful. "You leave it to me. Just tell me when you're prepared to consult with Dabashi, uh, Superior Dabashi. I'll bring him to you and find reasons to interrupt should his consultation go long. How does that sound?"

Michael could not have hoped for a better outcome. And he seemed to have accidentally formed a common bond with Guteerez, who almost forgot to say Dabashi's title when speaking to a Monk.

"That sounds very generous, Superior," Michael said.

"Good. Now. Let's have a celebratory post-meal ale, shall we?"

CHAPTER 7

"But I was assigned to find things exactly like this!" Corge tried not to shout. "Why would it need to wait?"

"Ibrahima has a very busy schedule, Corge. She can't just drop everything to meet with everyone who wants to." Ibrahima's assistant, Generalist Yao-wei said. If Corge hadn't been so agitated, he would have noticed the remarkable calm the assistant maintained and probably would have guessed that Yao-wei dealt with this a lot.

"So what am I supposed to do? Just hold off on what may be the most important discovery ever until an appointment opens up in a few weeks?" Corge realized he sounded obnoxious, even to himself. "I'm sorry. That was ridiculously pompous," he hastened to add. "And I know you don't know me, but I don't talk like that and I hate people who do, and I don't talk like that so much that I don't even say it about the people who do talk like that, so I can only assure you that it would take something incredibly important to make me talk like that."

Yao-wei just smiled. Corge assumed he was about to get thrown out.

"It's OK, Corge. It's a small station. I know you're not a Tripathi or anything. Hold on a second," he turned to go into Ibrahima's lab and then turned back. "Don't go anywhere but—don't do anything either. Promise?"

"Promise."

Yao-wei disappeared into the lab. Nobody in the small settlement of Armstrong had a private office; even Executives timeshared. But Ibrahima was one of the few who had a private space. The Earth Communications lab she occupied was often staffed by multiple people, but because of its sensitive nature and the risk misunderstandings could cause, Ibrahima had the right to use it exclusively. And she often did.

Yao-wei came back out and said, "Ibrahima will see you now," and held the door open.

Corge stood, stunned, still clutching the paper he carried all the way from the café.

"Go!" Yao-wei motioned. Corge finally began to move toward the door. Yao-wei stopped him right before he went in. "You owe me. Make it a good discovery, or I'm in the doghouse."

Corge looked puzzled.

"Old expression. Now don't keep her waiting."

Corge walked in.

The laboratory seemed like it should be bigger from the outside. In fact, it wasn't that much bigger than the chamber Yao-wei occupied. Corge was used to small rooms on the station, so he rarely noticed size. For some reason, in this case he had assumed there would be an exception, maybe because Ibrahima was an exception in so many other ways.

The lab was long and narrow. A bar ran along the left side as you walked in and contained various monitors and input devices, some extraordinarily rare. Most of the equipment looked like it came from the time of the Disconnection. Corge even noticed an example of a manual pointing device. It had been nicknamed after an animal, but he couldn't remember which one. A rat?

On the right side were a series of workbenches with more up-to-date Armstrong refurbishments. Not much new was manufactured on Armstrong, of course, but older materials were constantly getting reused and recycled in new configurations. The workbenches showed projects in various states of progress, including a translation database reconstruction and a particle detector as well as some historical research.

At the end of the room, shoved into a corner underneath an overhang of pipes and vents, was Ibrahima's desk. She sat in her chair, turned away from her work toward the entrance, and watched him walk the whole way in until he was right in front of her.

"Yes?" she asked.

"We have to send a message to New York."

"Is that all?"

It was not the reaction Corge was expecting. "Well there's more on why. You see, the Archive we found is empty because the physical—"

"Because the physical backup never arrived, but a remote backup may have been attempted in New York," she interrupted him.

"Yes," was all Corge could think to say.

"Right. You're new at this, so I'm going to try not to rip your head off and throw it, and your remaining corpse, out the airlock. From now on, before you go shouting about the next call we're going to make to Earth, come check records here. We already have, in our very own database, a record of attempts to preserve knowledge in NYC and here. Most of it was encrypted, and it took a long time to decipher. But we know some of it. The missing part was SLC, which you saw on the paper.

"The other amazing thing is that we have computers. And you scanned the paper. Which means I have been looking at it too and came to a similar conclusion." Ibrahima was much meaner in person, Corge thought.

"Now. I'm going to pretend that you didn't shout improper and frankly confidential things in the café. I'm going to pretend you didn't somehow flatter Yao-wei into convincing me you were an earnest and possibly genius Observer who was worth interrupting my current research. And I'm going to pretend you are coming to me at an appointed time with a clear presentation that you haven't told anyone else about," she took a deep breath, smiled and looked him in the eyes. "What do you have, Corge?"

At first, he could barely talk, but as he got going he realized he really did have something. When he began to compare his theory to hers, he found his was much more developed. She hadn't thought about the three-way system the way he had with SLC as the prime location. She also hadn't thought of messaging the people of New York rather than the Archive.

"Why not just try to send a point to point from the machine we have?" Ibrahima asked, all traces of her earlier condescension and sarcasm gone.

"We could do that and maybe should. I jumped over that. But my guess is that they may not have a working Archive. What if they have a shell like ours? A point to point may work, but it wouldn't return any information. And," he looked around as if someone might be listening.

"It's OK," Ibrahima said, a note of unusual gentleness in her voice. "You're doing it right this time. You can say whatever's on your mind."

"Right. What if there isn't anyone alive down there? We'll get confirmation of signal received but that could just mean the NYC Archive wasn't destroyed and it's been sitting down there on solar power in a dead land. I think we should send a readable message. See if they indicate that a human read it."

Ibrahima frowned. "What if it's just an AI that answers? How do we know?"

"Turing test," answered Corge without thinking.

"A what?"

Corge thought she was joking with him again. "A Turing test. It's a way of telling if an AI is actually sentient or not. There's no record of sentient AIs in any of our Citadelian Records—that I know of—so it's a good bet if it passes a Turing test, it's human."

Ibrahima grinned. "Clever boy. I think I may have heard the phrase 'Turing test' before. It's pretty old. Like talking about animalcules instead of viruses and bacteria. What I do know something about is the Lanier Range. It's a quick scale that's 90 percent accurate at judging an AI. Hadn't thought about it for this, but it would apply."

Corge just stared.

"And no," Ibrahima continued, "we don't have any secret records of sentient AIs on Earth or here. No records of alien contact or Moon mole men either!"

"You're making fun of me," Corge said flatly.

"A little. But good work. Seriously. Don't fuck up again and shout things like this to the world but DO bring them to me even if you think they're ridiculous. This is going to kick up a Coriolis cloud."

"Why?" Corge asked.

"Because, based on this, I'm going to recommend to the Executive Council that we use the machine to attempt to send a human-readable message to Earth, targeted to NYC."

"Why will that cause a problem? Isn't there a standard beacon attempting communication all the time?"

"That's pretty much what the controversy will be about," Ibrahima sighed. "Resources will say we shouldn't waste power on a separate transmission when we could just listen instead. Psychology will say any attempt to target a contact will raise hope to dangerously high levels and risk backlash. History will come up with 15,000 reasons NYC wouldn't, couldn't or shouldn't answer us. And the Executive Council will only worry about what public opinion will say if the message isn't answered, which it likely won't be."

"Oh," was all Corge could muster. "So why try?"

"Because I like the impossible. And I think they're all wrong and you're right. I want you there. Create a real presentation brief, based on what we hashed out here. Submit it to Yao-wei tomorrow and I'll touch it up. I'll copresent with you and we'll tag team the questions. You just answer facts, and I'll back you up with persuasion. Sound good?"

Corge swallowed hard. "You want me to copresent this with you to the Executive Council?"

"The most controversial Specialist in the known world with the most recent superstar. Should be a dynamite ticket. Don't worry. You just survived this. You'll do fine. Now go before I change my mind about the airlock. Yao-wei already knows. I just messaged him. So get to work!"

CAPITULUM 3

Michael dreaded the next hour and at the same time was elated. It interfered with his concentration. He had to focus. If the control box was not in the proper state when Dabashi arrived, the whole scheme would be for nothing. Michael doubted he would get a second attempt.

It was too late to delay. Guteerez promised Dabashi would stop by the Reliquary this afternoon and look in on Michael's progress.

He'd been so busy preparing for his encounter with Dabashi that he barely had time for any new work. That didn't matter much to him. Without being able to access the control box, he couldn't discover much anyway.

He managed to find a sort of manual on the screen and learned the basics of the system's ciphering scheme. Even that, he only knew in outline. Anything more required authentication.

Michael feared the box would lock him out if he tried and failed to authenticate himself. He'd seen a few examples of ancient devices that broke or become unusable after asking for identification a certain number of times. Either the control box of the Sculpture didn't work that way, or he'd been lucky and not tripped its particular self-defense mechanism.

He spent most of his time testing the right configuration. He thought he had it but he would only know for sure once Dabashi authenticated it, if the Superior actually could. There was always a chance that the Dabashi mentioned on the paper artifact had nothing to do with a person of any kind, much less the Superior of the New York Citadel by the same name.

But it was worth a try. Michael followed the instructions as best he could. He found the proper communication authentication scheme setting. His plan was to get it to the point of only having to enact one selection to authenticate and then ask Superior Dabashi to help interpret what it meant.

Then, while they were looking at it, Michael would "accidentally" make the selection. Dabashi's presence would authenticate, hopefully. Then Guteerez would interrupt and call him away before he could see what had happened. If all went well, Dabashi would only think Michael was an idiot who couldn't make a fairly easy translation of a Citadelian relic, and Michael would have the access he needed to the machine.

Michael heard footsteps. He got the selection screen in the proper state as Dabashi and Guteerez walked in.

"Here is the Superior, Michael. I hope you have a worthwhile problem for him. The Superior is very busy." From a step behind Dabashi, Superior Guteerez rolled his eyes as he said this.

"Yes, what is it, Michael?" snapped Dabashi. "I've been reading your reports. I can't say I've seen anything revelatory in your work. I hope this won't waste my time. You do know how to properly operate a touchscreen, don't you?"

Michael had no idea what a touchscreen was, but he did know he had to touch the control box display to make it work. So he just nodded.

"I'll leave you two to it," said Guteerez and left.

Dabashi sighed. "We'll let's have it. What's this unsolvable issue that requires my valuable time to get past so you can continue to waste your own time unimpeded?"

The Superior wasn't making it easy. Michael could barely speak. He motioned for Dabashi to come to the control box. "It's this selection here."

"Selection? Where did you learn that terminology?"

"It's in my Heretic-loving reports," Michael stopped himself from saying. Instead, he said, "I picked up the term from some of the manual pages I've been reporting about." It was as close to accusing Dabashi of not reading the reports as Michael dared.

Dabashi grunted. "Ah. I skipped past most of that. Frighteningly boring. You might consider skipping it yourself and possibly important things won't be missed in future."

Michael very carefully did not punch Dabashi square in the nose and continued. "I understand this first part that indicates an advance to a new state requiring input. And I can read the basic yes-no response, of course. But what does the question line actually mean?"

Michael chose this question because it was honest. He really didn't know what the line literally meant. He knew from the paper what it generally indicated and what it would do, but not what it meant.

"Hmm," Dabashi grunted. "Well, I think it's obvious, but then I can read it. And even if it's obvious, I do respect your attention to detail."

Dabashi stopped and looked at Michael. His grim expression didn't change an ounce but his tone softened a small amount. It was more positive emotion than Michael had ever witnessed from the Superior.

"You probably think I just want to get in your way, Michael. I do not. I have no need or desire to explain why. However, I have read your reports and, in amongst the drivel and the wasted paragraphs, you show some intelligence. I—I just wanted you to know that." He turned back to the control box. "As you have rightly noticed, most text is in an understandable, if archaic, language. But some lines are written in Symbology. Many think—and I am certain—this was meant to restrict the understanding, or at least the speed, of those not trained in its operation. I have learned the Symbolics language.

"Stated properly, it's not actually a language. It merely represents the words with other symbols. These here mean 'Select, Authentication, Present Multiple.' It doesn't have the same syntax as our speech or even ancient speech, but it essentially means, 'press this button to identify anyone who should be using this machine and begin using it.'"

This was it. Michael paused for a moment, waiting for Guteerez to come in and distract Dabashi. But Guteerez did not arrive.

"Do you understand?" Dabashi's harshness had returned.

"Yes, I think so. So when the operators of old would get to this point, they would have to be authenticated to proceed?" Michael kept looking toward the door.

"Stop being distracted by whatever's passing by in the corridor! But yes. You have it right. Even down to the appropriate word, 'authenticated.' You must have picked that up in your famous manuals again. You are a quick study, Michael."

Michael needed more time. "What would happen next?"

"Nothing if you weren't properly identified, most likely. If you were 'authenticated,' as you say, you would be taken into a menu of operation options of some sort."

Michael knew better. Dabashi wasn't wrong. But Michael knew it wasn't just an operations menu of some sort. It was the operations menu for the Communications Assembly of the Sculpture. Either

Dabashi couldn't recognize this selection as specific to communications, or he wasn't letting on that he knew.

"Here, watch," Dabashi said. To Michael's horror, he selected the affirmative and advanced the program. The selection moved to a Symbology map for communications options that Michael recognized from some manual pages he had unlocked. He stifled a gasp.

Dabashi seemed unfazed. "This is for communications of some sort. Probably with a command center or coordinating body. This first one is for message entry and—this is interesting. Some of these characters—"

Guteerez finally arrived, out of breath.

"Superior Dabashi, my apologies. But you're needed by Superior Akhtar in the Atmospherics Reliquary."

Dabashi seemed torn. "Of course," he muttered. "They barely know what oxygen is without me there to point it out for them. Michael, take what you learned from me here and get me a report specifically on that screen. I mean selection. You know what I mean. There are some interesting Symbologies there I want explored."

Dabashi hurried out of the room. Guteerez remained.

"My apologies, Michael, but I was delayed by Superior Akhtar. It took some work to persuade him to accept Superior Dabashi's help. Apparently, the staff in Atmospherics isn't as keen for him to assist them as he may think."

Michael just stared in panic. He couldn't believe that a crisis had not occurred. That he still stood there in the Reliquary with the Sculpture, unpunished, unspoiled, with his plan in shreds but its hoped-for outcome still intact. He reached for the screen and selected the symbol that meant "generate" to create a message.

"Here, what are you doing, Michael?" Guteerez stepped toward him in view of the control box. He spoke in a low, almost menacing tone. "Before you proceed one more selection, tell me what you have discovered and how much Dabashi knows about it."

Michael stopped and looked wide-eyed at Guteerez.

"What do you mean? Our agreement didn't involve that."

"Didn't involve what, Michael? Our agreement, frankly, is whatever I say it is. You hold no power here. Please don't forget that. Even so, I'm not threatening you," he held his hands up and grinned. "I'm merely curious."

Michael hesitated. "Do you promise you will keep it secret and not shut me down?"

"I promise, Michael," Guteerez said, lowering his hands and placing one on Michael's shoulders, "that I want what you want. But don't verge on threatening a Superior, my boy. It's not a good practice to get into. Now tell me. Everything."

So Michael told him everything. Almost.

CHAPTER 8

"In summary, this new information provided by Corge raises the I value in Radic's equation by a level of two. It raises the R value by three factors and with other small adjustments, our overall contact chance estimate rises a full point," Ibrahima held them in the palm of her hand. Corge couldn't believe anyone would oppose her.

"While we all know that chance remains infinitesimally small, the resource cost expressed in station lifespan reduction is even smaller. For almost no cost to the longevity of the station, we have the greatest chance since Disconnection to communicate with Earth."

Silence. She had said the great taboo, the great unsayable. Communicate. With. Earth. That was the big bet here and she was now all in. She had strategically opened the way for the biggest objection. She explained to Corge that it was better to get it out early so opposition would lose energy over the course of the discussion. It was some kind of communications theory principle that Corge didn't fully understand.

As polite applause died down in the Assembly, LeAnn whispered in Corge's ear, "Here comes the shitstorm."

The first line of questioning came from the Resources Committee. Its representative was a small man called Narayan who spoke in a curiously high voice that was still undeniably masculine.

"Ibrahima, thank you for all your work. Nobody here needs a repeat of our remedial explanation of resource management in Armstrong. But given those well-known constraints, why not just monitor for signals? We have always done so of course, but it has been such a wide spectrum. It seems that any NYC or SLC teams that might exist would have a far better chance of knowing about the Moon Archive than we would have had of discovering it here. And if they are active and advanced enough to help us, they would likely signal us. Now that we know the frequency and encryption, would it not be wiser and more efficient to wait for their call?"

Corge got ready to be called upon. Ibrahima had prepared him and LeAnn both to be ready at any moment to provide testimony. Corge, obviously, could speak to the discovery of the device and what it might mean. LeAnn's knowledge of the location and logistics of the machinery might come into play as well.

But Ibrahima didn't even look at them. "That would make sense if we thought some shred of the civilization of the Citadels had survived the assault of the Heretics." Only Ibrahima could skate this close to offensive speculation about Earth and come away unscathed. "But if you discuss this with our esteemed Psychology Specialists, you'll find that it's likely that much of civilization was lost and wiped away. A less sensitive example comes from ancient Rome. Its knowledge was vast for its time, but when Europe fell, much was lost, even with the church protecting Rome and Constantinople. In fact, some argue so much was lost specifically because the church played such an active role in the latter days of the Empire.

"So it's perfectly logical to think that we have the only continuous history and only continuous knowledge in humanity. And if that is the case, and we only now discovered this Archive and learned only a slice of its secrets, then by just listening, we may listen forever. Or would if we could."

Corge winced at that last jab, which implied that following the Resources line of thinking would doom the station to eventual failure. It was just this side of tasteless. The insult was not lost on the representative from Resources who sat down without thanking Ibrahima.

Roger Hu was the next to speak for the Psychology committee. Corge realized that Ibrahima had just used them to defend herself. It was a gambit partly meant to sway them to her side, but he wondered if it came off as patronizing or presumptive.

"Thank you, Ibrahima, for your accurate understanding of our discipline," Hu began. Corge couldn't tell if he was sincere or mocking—his tone was perfectly even.

"What a dick," LeAnn whispered. It was clear how she interpreted it.

"We are very pleased that the proceedings of this chamber are on delayed release, giving you the security to speak frankly. It is a benefit to all our understanding."

"Yep," Corge whispered back to LeAnn, and she laughed.

"However, a contact plan, as you suggest, could not be reasonably kept from general knowledge. And as we all know too well from our early history, any publicized or unusual attempt at contact beyond our current sustained attempts can raise hopefulness to a level that is dangerous if not fulfilled. Can you guarantee a response?" He raised an eyebrow.

"Thank you, Hu," Ibrahima shot back, her words not matching her biting tone, which Corge had only heard her use in her own lab. "While I know just the smallest bit of your discipline—enough to quote you directly and appropriately—I do not practice your branch of the discipline. If another asked this question, I would call upon you to answer it. If we attempt to contact the SLC or NYC Archives, would it risk a 94 situation?"

She had deftly turned the tables on him, but he was not backing down. "The chances of a repeat of 94 are small, of course, however the danger of a retrograde backlash would be close to 50 percent—"

"How close?" Ibrahima interrupted. This finally threw him off guard.

"We have not run a formal analysis, but my estimates would say close to—"

She cut him off again. "So you don't know."

"I will run the numbers and submit them."

He sat down quickly but still with no visible show of anger or resentment. He snapped a quick command to an assistant who ran off as if he were charged with getting the numbers before the session ended.

Next up was the representative from the History division, Mr. Jun.

"Ibrahima, we've discussed this at length, so I'll forego the questioning and make a brief statement."

LeAnn snorted.

"What?" Corge whispered.

"Mr. Jun never does anything short. If it's really his idea of short, we'll still be here all day."

She wasn't kidding. He began with what he described as a brief account of the conditions of the Fall, recounting the history of how the Citadels had brought stability to human society and the Heretics rebelled against it. How the Heretics claimed that stability was stifling humanity and the only cure was to bring down society and start again. He told them the story they all knew too well about how the Armstrong Station, staffed by scientists and industrial workers, had been cut off by the swiftness of the Disconnection.

He then moved into speculation of what his History team thought likely must have happened next.

LeAnn sighed. "Finally something at least some of us don't already know."

"Psychology is best at assessing the probabilities, of course, but the trends of history bear out the conclusion that it is unlikely that any Citadel has preserved its full functioning. In a secret endeavor like this, it is more than likely that all knowledge on the surface has been lost."

"The surface?" Corge asked LeAnn.

"Yeah, it's an old term for Earth. Dates back to the old record-keeping pre-Disconnection. Since we're on the Moon, everything was written with a return journey in mind, and the surface was always Earth. It was a way of looking at Armstrong like a big orbiting satellite, which in a way it really is since it's on Earth's biggest satellite."

Corge had never thought of that. In his mind, like most station-dwellers, Armstrong was an outpost of humanity, cut off from the tribe and hoping to reconnect. This other view implied that humanity hadn't seen Armstrong that way before the Fall, that Armstrong was an experiment or a utility running "up there" and, in some sense, expendable. He stopped thinking and paid attention as Mr. Jun began wrapping up.

"So Ibrahima has convinced me that, despite these low probabilities, the fact that they are probabilities at all justifies the low expenditure of resources to test them. Thank you."

Corge noticed he hadn't exceeded his allotted time, but he certainly had made full use of it. No time wasted taking questions.

The Council asked for open comments but, as was typical, none were given. The Council had a good record of finding the representatives of actual differences of opinion and calling on them, leaving no need for any other comments in most cases. The Armstrong taboo against waste kept most people from repeating arguments.

Serafina, the representative of the Executive Committee, stood for the final statements. The Executive Committee always got the last chance to speak. Corge wondered if he might get away without having to answer any questions.

"Here come our grillings," said LeAnn.

Before he had a chance to react to this, Serafina called upon him.

"If Generalist Corge would be so kind as to tell us the nature of the material on which he found the manual page?"

Corge stood, spluttering. "The material? It was paper." A shuddering noise rolled through the audience. He couldn't tell if it was laughter or disapproval. "A rag weave, according to analysis."

"Where is it located now?"

"In the Communications lab. In Ibrahima's lab."

"Why has it not been recycled?"

"It may be soon. I think. I believe it is better to read it as discovered. Sometimes it makes the meaning clearer." He felt like an idiot saying it out loud.

"Just so. Thank you, Corge. Specialist LeAnn, what condition is the machine in?" Serafina asked.

Corge saw that LeAnn had gone from mild amusement to befuddlement.

"Condition? High-grade solar degradation externally but working condition, with refurbishment underneath."

"And why has it not been recycled?"

"Are you nuts?" LeAnn spat back.

"I assure you, Specialist LeAnn, I am not. Please explain why it has not been recycled. All found items are of such rarity that all must be recycled except in great need."

"There's great need. Both of study and education and possible use for return communication."

"But the return communication need is not determinative in the decision?"

LeAnn collected herself. "No, it is only one factor in Reclamations assessment."

"Thank you, Specialist LeAnn," said Serafina. Ibrahima shot LeAnn a glare of shock and amusement.

"Fellow committee members, I believe we have all the facts we need to make our assessment. If you will permit me, I'd like to lay out suggested parameters for our vote. Members of the committee who take a viewpoint often referred to as the Passive view believe we should always favor listening over acting. More aggressive beliefs, of course, differ. I believe we should gauge what effect any action we take will have on public opinion."

Serafina turned toward the committee members with what Corge felt must have been a dramatic attempt at a steely glare. It made her look less persuasive in his eyes, as if she were play-acting. But he knew little of Executive interactions. Maybe this sort of thing worked.

"This is a most divisive and dangerous issue, whether we get an answer or not. Think of three scenarios. In the first scenario, the people of the station learn all the details of the Archive and that we have done nothing. In the second scenario, we attempt communication but receive no answer. In the third scenario, we attempt communication and receive an answer. How will the initial reaction, and the resulting sway of hopes, change the dynamics on the station? For your convenience, the Psychology department has informally modeled these scenarios under the advisement of History and Logistics. You will find them in your inbox.

"Finally, I ask you to review this," a reproduction of a page from an old encyclopedia showed up on their screens, detailing the Citadel system. "That is what existed before Disconnection. That is what fell. Ponder what kind of society might have arisen from those ashes. Ponder whether we want to force it to communicate before it's ready or whether we want to wait until it feels it needs us. Peril lies in both directions. But we must do our best. Thank you."

Leann stood and stretched. Most of the people in the chamber did the same. "I'm getting coffee from the café. Do you want some?" she asked Corge.

"Yes," he said, staying seated. "I'll catch up with you. I want to look at this encyclopedia page. I don't think I've ever seen it. Have you?"

"No," LeAnn yawned. "But it didn't look much different than the current standard one to me."

"It is," said Corge his voice trailing off. "It mentions us from the outside. From Earth's perspective. We never let ourselves see that."

LeAnn looked puzzled. "Why does it matter?"

"I'm not sure," Corge said, rubbing his chin. "But it does. Otherwise this would be in the general database instead of hidden in reserve banks until needed in a highly divisive fight for the future of Armstrong."

"Well, when you put it that way—"

"That's why I want to look at it. Thanks for getting the coffee."

"Right. Coffee. I'll be right back. Don't have any world-changing revelations without me."

Corge didn't say anything. He was lost in the vagaries of the encyclopedia page.

Aggregate Wikibase – Inter-Citadel Edition – Accessed 20/21313/465 – Armstrong@cit32

The Citadels
A description of The Aggregate of the 31 Citadels and a brief history.

Edited by Jacki Kim – Written by Crowd

The Aggregate of the 31 Citadels is most often attributed to the decline in population. In ancient times, as the population of the planet swelled unnaturally, people moved into cities that grew into monstrous megaplexes of sprawling humanity.

When population declined, it struck hardest at the countryside. Cities became livable as they became less crowded. The majority of the population stayed urban. Hints of this effect had been seen in the many economic downturns experienced during the times of rising population. While jobs may have been lost for some, most found that housing became more affordable, services became kinder and crowding became less of a problem.

The population decline meant that growth no longer drove the economy. Cheap labor could no longer fuel that unchecked growth. Instead, sustainability moved from being a laudable goal to the essential means for business to survive.

Cities provided the infrastructure and economies of scale necessary to support sustainable business. As population receded from high tide, the remainder washed up into large cities. Eventually, 31 population centers took the lead over the small villages and museum cities left behind.

Raising of the Citadels

The Citadel Movement recognized the importance of the remaining viable cities as part of an agglomeration that succeeded nation-states as the dominant units of government. Nations still exist, of course, as representative agencies for special interests but are not the governing powers they were long ago. Cities rose from subservient to centralized powers to become the centers of power themselves. To formalize this new, more effective power, the Citadel Movement began.

The movement grew out of a separation of responsibility. In most of the 31 cities, an older form of Executive who was subservient to national power, usually a mayor, transitioned into a ceremonial post. The Executive's seat remained in city halls. New Executives rose out of regional bodies that ruled the real metropolis, not the antiquated borders set down long ago and blurred by sprawl. These new managers distinguished their offices by calling them citadels. The name indicated this was the government of the entire population in an urban area, not only of one arbitrary section.

For instance, in New York, the mayor continued to reign over the five boroughs of New York City from the city hall in Manhattan. But the tri-state ombudsman rose to prominence in his offices in the Empire State Building, which eventually became the New York Citadel, covering New Jersey, Connecticut and Long Island as well as the five boroughs.

The first Citadel rose in Shenzhen in a new building created by the People's Party for the regional commander. As cities began to imitate this model, some created buildings, while others, like New York, named an existing building as their Citadel. A few, because of quirks in geography, have adopted a rotating Citadel that moves every few years into a new building. The Lagos Citadel operates under this model. In all cases, citizens identify themselves by what Citadel they are from. Those few left in smaller towns like Madrid or Chicago, for instance, identify with the nearest Citadel. Others call themselves "farmers," a term derived from ancient agriculture workers, used to mean anyone living outside of the direct governance of the 31.

As the 31 great Citadels formed, they instituted "The Aggregate" to coordinate their efforts when cooperation was needed and resolve or avoid conflicts. All Citadels value cooperation and sustainability above all else and The Aggregate makes that possible. The Aggregate of the 31 Citadels has achieved the most stable and sustainable prosperity ever achieved in human history.

Honorary Citadels

When speaking of the rise of the 31 Citadels, it is worth noting that two communities are commonly referred to as Citadels though they are not part of The Aggregate of 31. One is the Antarctic Citadel, built in celebration of the 100th anniversary of the founding of The Aggregate. It is the tallest structure in Antarctica and houses the Chief Research Scientist of the International Academy of Scientists' mission to the continent. It also provides excellent labs and resources for research as well as several luxury hotels. However, there is no permanent population on Antarctica, and as such, it has not requested nor required representation in the 31.

The other community of note is the Lunar Citadel of Armstrong, built by the Space Agency in the early days of the 31. Some older texts refer to it as Citadel 32 and to The Aggregate as "The 32," showing how high hopes ran that the Moon would become a full-fledged civilization.

Sadly the dream was never realized and references to "The 32" merely date the text in question. The Citadel in Armstrong houses a local government for both Lunar and Martian activities but hosts no permanent representatives from the 31 because there is no native population. The occupants of Armstrong consist entirely of international science and commercial representatives drawn from the 31 Citadels of Earth, none of whom are permanent residents.

Both the Lunar and Antarctic Citadels have honorary but nonvoting seats in the meetings of the 31. The Lunar representative rarely attends. The Antarctic mission sends a scientist from their Citadel as an honor in recognition of scientific achievement.

Corge was explaining his interpretation of the page to LeAnn when Ibrahima walked up.

"We're a novelty," Corge said. "Why would they contact us? If you go by the tone of this, the only reason they even located an Archive here was because it was out of the way and had some people to watch over it. Armstrong is the janitorial closet and we're the janitors. When the building collapses, you don't go running back in to find the closet. They don't want to find us. They don't care. Or at least they won't care until civilization recovers enough to allow dilettantes to search for our remains, like explorers looking for Atlantis. We can't afford to wait for that!"

"So you figured out Serafina's gamble then," Ibrahima said, walking up with a cup of coffee of her own in hand. "Her words leaned subtly toward the Passives, which is all to the good, as they are the more volatile element and more likely to get defensive. But her evidence struck squarely in support of the Contactists. That's us, by the way. Certainly you, Corge. You verge on sounding like a Returnist," Ibrahima laughed.

Corge thought Ibrahima meant it as a joke, but it also served as a warning that he might be overreacting a bit. Returnists advocated using all of Armstrong's resources to build a rocket that would return them all to Earth. Aside from the near impossibility of creating a space-worthy vessel big enough for the Armstrong population, it also ignored the fact that no recovery teams would assist them when they landed. The Armstrong contingent wouldn't last long in Earth gravity with no modern medicine to recuperate them. That was the biggest argument against even small return vessels—that, and the perceived waste of resources.

"I'm not a Returnist," he tried to laugh. "But I do find this encyclopedia page pretty damning. We were a freaking tourist attraction before Disconnection. There's not much reason to assume our value in the fight for survival down there, if that's our legacy. We're a curiosity."

"So many think," Ibrahima sighed. "But I doubt it. I think our legend grows from this. That's what the Passives will assert. They're doing it on their private debate board right now. I peeked. They argue Armstrong would gain a mystical status in post-Disconnection societies and be presumed to contain all the mysteries of civilization before the Disconnection. Finding us would be essential to getting society back on its feet. At least, that's their argument. And I can't say I disagree."

"Why does it matter?" asked LeAnn between sips of coffee. "I mean, it seems simple to me. We send the message and see what happens. We're pretty tough after all these years, right? We can take a little disappointment."

"You're not wrong in the short term," said Ibrahima. "But we're in the business of estimating the effect of a butterfly flapping its wings."

"A what?" LeAnn asked.

"You never learned about the butterfly in physics?" asked Corge, surprised. "That was one of my favorite lessons. Mr. Kapoor had some cool demos of small causes leading to huge effects. I remember this one with Ping-Pong balls and tubing—"

"Oh, that crap," said LeAnn. "I remember being incredibly bored by that. I was way more into the practical physics. I think I may have skipped some of the demos to do extra credit in mechanics lessons."

Corge and Ibrahima just stared at LeAnn.

"What?" she said.

"You skipped demos? The most fun thing in all Student levels?" Corge gaped.

"Your assignment was never in doubt, was it?" said Ibrahima.

"I think the delivery doctor made her a Specialist in tunnel maintenance," Corge joked, still somewhat slack-jawed. This made Ibrahima chuckle.

LeAnn refused to take the bait. "Whatever. You can have your boring fantasies. That's why we're in this Assembly. A bunch of people who think too much, who liked doing demos instead of dealing with reality."

Corge spoke gently. "Sorry, LeAnn. Didn't mean to tease. But the butterfly effect is practical. It's just long term. It's like a small drip from a water return conduit that would eventually lose us gallons of our water. It's a small drip, but you want to stop it, right?"

LeAnn didn't want to let go of her annoyance, but she let Corge lead her anyway. "Of course."

"So the disappointment from a failed response is like a small leak. If the leak is necessary to make sure our plants get watered in time for harvest, we live with it and fix it afterward, right?"

"Maybe," she begrudged.

"Otherwise, you fix the leak right away, even if you have to shut off water for a while."

"OK."

"Well, the transmission is a drip. It won't cause immediate revolution. But it could destabilize the psychology of the station, which even someone as practical as you knows is fragile. So are we watering plants or not? That's what's up for debate."

"You know, Corge, you're a real jerk," laughed LeAnn. "You just made me understand the butterfly effect."

Ibrahima placed a hand on Corge's shoulder. "That was impressive."

Before she could continue, the members of the Assembly began returning for the vote. "Here we go," she said, and headed back to her seat.

It didn't take very long. A culture like Armstrong's learned to be efficient at everything, even bureaucracy. A constant threat against survival proved to be one way of making government work.

Each Executive in the Assembly approached Serafina, who registered their vote and allowed them to verify it. The vote would go into the record, normally made public immediately. This session would only become public right away if the decision to transmit was supported. After the last vote was registered, Serafina waited for the Executive to return to her seat. Serafina would only vote in case of a tie.

"Does anyone object to the vote?" she asked the chamber.

Silence.

"Then it will be considered a binding decision of every person here. The vote favors transmission. Ibrahima is charged with overseeing the procedure. Roger Hu will carry out messaging. That is all."

"Outrage!" one of the Passives yelled. A few members stopped and looked stunned at the outburst.

"Is that normal?" Corge whispered to LeAnn. She shrugged and looked as surprised as he felt.

Serafina had already turned to leave the chamber, paused and turned back. She had a very genuine and very real version of the steely glare she had pretended earlier in the day.

"The decision. Is binding. On every person here."

Corge heard malice in every word. The unspoken threat almost overpowered the meaning of the statement. Ibrahima rose and moved toward Serafina. Most of the chamber had been leaving but now stopped.

More Passives began to gather together, shouting.

"Madness!"

"You'll wreck us all!"

"It's suicide!"

"STOP!" Serafina shouted. "I call for an emergency reassembly. NOW!"

"I think I know why she was chosen as Assembly Leader," whispered LeAnn. She and Corge both fell quickly into their seats at her shout. The Assembly itself rapidly returned to sit down and Corge experienced the most awkward silence ever.

"You don't agree with the decision." Serafina spoke calmly, but her rage and fire simmered underneath. "You seem to imply it is dangerous. Is it more dangerous than overturning our system of government? Are you Students who cry when a referee's call in their games goes against them? Do you somehow feel that you are the only privileged members who understand the world, and the rest of your co-citizens are imbeciles?

"For that is how it appears. I call a vote of censure." An audible gasp came from the Assembly. Even Corge knew censure from the Assembly was an accusation of a serious crime almost on the level of wasting resources. The few who had ever been censured were effectively ruined. Not a small punishment in a society as small and closed as Armstrong.

The Passives who had begun the shouting earlier looked shocked and angered and were beginning to stand. Ibrahima seemed about to rise to object when Serafina continued.

"The subject of potential censure is myself. Voice vote. I can only assume that my incompetence did not allow for a full and fair discussion of the issue. Therefore I call censure on myself. All in favor?"

Not a squeak. Not a chair moved. Nobody coughed. Even the air vents seemed unusually quiet.

"Opposed?" A firm but somewhat muted "No," rumbled through the chamber.

"That's settled. Emergency Assembly adjourned. Let's have no more unpleasantness."

"Brilliant," mused Corge.

"More like stupid," said LeAnn. "What if they'd voted yes?"

"Not a chance," said Corge. "Only the Passives would even have thought about it, and she gave them no time to think. She gambled, very safely in my opinion, that they wouldn't be mad enough to ruin her life over this, especially without consideration, and she gave them none. She just avoided weeks of problems."

"Maybe," said Ibrahima, walking up and overhearing the last of what Corge said. "Or she may have just brought a simmer to a boil. I think the stove's still hot, in any case. Expect a more subtle opposition now, but expect it nonetheless, Corge. Come. We have work to do."

CAPITULUM 4

Michael had told Guteerez almost everything. Almost. He expected there would be an encryption scheme to break after authorization, and he had been right. He only hinted at that vaguely in his talk with Guteerez.

What he couldn't have known when he talked to Guteerez was that he would stumble on the decryption key and break it so easily. He marveled at the brilliant simplicity of the key.

Michael loved the ancient things that filled the Reliquary. He loved to imagine the past when those things were new. Before he began spending all his time in the Sculpture's room, he had spent time exploring another room with artifacts from the Metalwork Age. That age encompassed the first widespread forging of metals up to the first widespread manufacture of complex machinery. The first written records from that age came from civilizations like the Egyptian, Mesopotamian, Chinese, Mayan, Greek, Roman, Umayyad, Aztec and Incan.

He particularly liked the Rosetta Stone with its various languages and the story of how it was used to help decipher the meanings of the Egyptian hieroglyphs. He was inspired by that story when he discovered that the Sculpture's encryption used an old alphabet from the Electrical Age called Cyrillic. However, the letters made no sense, even in the languages known to have used that alphabet.

Taking a cue from the Rosetta Stone, he transliterated the Cyrillic into another alphabet, Greek, and then another alphabet, Latin. That didn't work. So he went from Cyrillic to Arabic to Latin. Then he tried a few more combinations, favoring ending in Latin because that was the alphabet most used by the Citadels.

He finally hit on it—Cyrillic to Greek to Manchu to Latin. The text became clear to read as anything written in his own time, albeit with some old-fashioned phrasing.

He hid his research materials and made himself memorize the Greek and Manchu alphabets before returning the books to the library. He didn't want anybody to know what he'd done. He had checked out the books with the alphabets along with several other historical texts so nobody could tell which books were important to his research.

Strangely, Dabashi had not been around to bother him. Guteerez only looked in to say hello and remind him to give the signal if he unlocked anything more. It had been ridiculously easy to hide his progress.

He decided to try entering an actual draft message and proceed right up to the transmission point. He hadn't yet dared pass beyond the "message creation" option. It made him nervous. He took a deep breath and bent his head down to the control box. He was exhausted. He was pushing himself too hard. He rested his forehead against the flat metal. It wasn't comfortable, but it still felt good to rest.

He woke with a jarring bump and the sound of a motor. He must have fallen asleep. He felt wind rushing by from outside. He opened his eyes to darkness, punctured by pinpoints of light floating in his vision. Was he sick? The points waved around, making him feel nauseated. His eyes adjusted and he realized he wasn't in the Reliquary anymore. In fact, he wasn't sure where he was.

He bounced again and felt the whole room he was in bounce with him. The wind wasn't blowing on him. It wasn't a breeze. It was coming in through the same places where the light was. He was in a cart. A tarp covered him, and he saw light coming through where it was tied to the sides of the cart.

His mouth felt dry and he had a splitting headache. He hadn't felt this bad since the last time he had the flu. The bouncing cart didn't help. The last thing he remembered was working at the control box near the Sculpture in the Reliquary. He tried to piece together anything else after that. He had heard a noise, maybe greeted some people, but he couldn't tease out any details. Every time he thought he had a clear memory, it escaped him.

Finally, the cart rolled to a stop and someone threw the canvas off. The sun hung low in the sky and blinded him. They must have spent most of the day rolling along. Two men with bandannas reached in through the blinding light and pulled him out. It felt like a dream.

"I'm a spaceman," he heard himself say to the bandanna men, and he felt like one. One of the men grunted a laugh and the other shushed him. He now understood the term "lightheaded." He'd never felt like this before. It really felt the way he imagined the people on the Moon must feel. Supposedly, gravity worked differently there and people were lighter. He bobbed along with the two men holding him firmly. He felt like they needed to hold him to keep him from floating away.

"Thank you," he said. Again, he spoke without meaning to.

At that moment, he noticed where he was, and it wasn't like anything he'd ever seen. He had never been outside New York's Citadel area. The farthest he'd ever been from Manhattan Island were short trips into the countryside to the east. A lovely farm in Queenlyn provided the fresh produce for the kitchens in the Complex. As a younger Monk, he had to go on several trips to bring the produce back in an autocart.

But that was a land of buildings amid grass. The gardens there grew among the ruins of the Citadelian civilization. While more open than Manhattan, it still had structure. It still looked like civilization, just a greener, sunnier and more open civilization than the island of the Citadel.

That was what he thought of as the country. This, where he had been taken against his will, was the wilderness. He dared to worry that it might even be the Devastation. The men led him toward a small metal shack with wavy walls. Could bombs have done that to walls? He still wasn't thinking clearly.

Other than the shack, nothing else was around in any direction. Not even trees. He saw some light green on the ground in the distance, though underfoot was only a coarse, grey gravel of some sort. Some plants lived out here but nothing big, and nothing numerous.

"It's almost dead," he muttered.

The grunting man openly laughed this time, and the other man reached in front of Michael to punch the grunter, snapping, "Shut up!" The man sounded irritated and mean.

The front of the metal shack was red with rust. The structure had four walls and a roof slapped together with whatever lay at hand without an ounce of effort spent on making things work well. A faded, red, plastic sheet hung there, tied to the metal on the left with rope in three places to serve as a door. On the right, a loop of black plastic attached the plastic sheet to a flap of metal cut out from the wall. This was shelter at its crudest.

The mean man worked the plastic loop while the grunting man held Michael. The lightheadedness had begun to fade during the walk and his headache roared back. He also felt the nausea return. He longed to be lightheaded again. As he settled into his body again, he felt a multitude of small agonies clamoring for his attention.

The mean man pulled the red, plastic flap back and the grunting man pulled Michael through the doorway. The room inside was roughly square. A hole had been cut out of the back to let in the light from the setting sun. In that dim light, Michael saw a wooden door set on a stack of logs to serve as a table along the wall on the left. He wondered why they didn't use the door as a door and have the plastic sheet serve as the tabletop. Too much work to make a real door work with the thin metal, he supposed.

On the makeshift table sat an unlighted fuel lamp. Its base was clear and Michael could see three quarters of the fuel was burned off. Several unmatched wooden and plastic chairs were scattered about the room. A huge, soft-looking blob of a material Michael had never seen before sat to the right near a battery heater. So these weren't Heretics. He had worried until he saw the heater. Heretics never touched battery devices. They would use electricity but only direct from the sun as they thought it the only pure source and self-limiting, as fit their theology.

A series of maps and charts hung on the metal walls, attached with some kind of adhesive Michael couldn't see. Some of the maps had red and yellow markers on them. He recognized the map of Manhattan and a marker indicating where the Citadel stood. The rest made no sense to him.

Aside from the two bandanna men who had brought him in, the only other person in the room was a withered old man with grey hair who sat in an odd, black plastic chair that seemed to have wheels under it. Who would want to sit in a chair that would move around under them? But the man sat quite well, spun around and wheeled over to them quite deftly.

Michael thought maybe the man was disabled until he stood and strode toward the three of them with his hand out.

"Welcome, Michael. I'm Jackson. Proud to meet you."

Michael just started at the hand. "Proud to meet you" was a greeting of the Heretic movement. What little remained of it.

"But you have a battery heater," Michael spluttered almost without meaning to. He was back in his own brain but not quite in full command of his faculties yet.

The man burst out laughing. "A phrase doesn't make a philosophy. I sympathize with many of the things the Heretics believe. But I don't sympathize with their lack of comforts when I can get them. I suppose that's confusing to a sheltered Monk like you who believes the world is being reordered by the Authority. Well, consider this the real beginning of your education, Michael."

"What are you?"

"I'm Jackson, I told you," He looked down. "You're not going to shake my hand?" he knitted his eyebrows in a look of worry. "Seems rude."

Michael let the man grab his hand in what felt more like coercion than greeting. Jackson worked Michael's arm like a puppet being worked by a master.

"Much better. Have a seat," Jackson motioned to one of the wooden chairs as he sat back in the black chair with wheels. "I know this isn't up to your usual standards of comfort, but it's all we have. The Authority may not consider us Heretics, but they don't allow us too many freedoms either. They don't like those of us who don't play along."

"But if you're not a Heretic and you don't work for the Authority, you're a Free Citizen. You must pay the support fees, certainly, but they are fair. Do you not work?"

Jackson began to laugh, but it faded into a grunt of anger. "No, Michael. We don't work. We steal. Why? Because, even though your Monk-addled brain will have a difficult time believing it, it gets us better accommodations than most so-called Free Citizens have."

Michael shook his head. "That's not true. I see Citizens every day in Manhattan—"

Jackson cut him off "Manhattan! Yes, and how do you get to live there? You already live there. Or you are related to someone who lives there. Or have a good relationship with a Superior or Factor or someone even higher up who lives there. You don't move there and find a place to live. Not unless you want to live in Queenlyn or Jorsey. Or risk your life refarming the South Island."

"Those aren't bad places. I've been to Queenlyn many times."

"Have you? To the Authority's farms, I bet. Oh yes. Sunny people in the sunny farms. But try buying food there as a Free Citizen. 'Farm it yourself!' they yell and drive you out. But on what land? No, they don't show you the outbuildings. The refuges. The camps. Free Citizens live in camps, Michael. Did you know that?"

"Of course," he said, feeling an unusual defensiveness for the order. "I've even visited one of the Jorsey campgrounds. It's a service for those transitioning to new ways of living. They provide shelter and education."

"Ha! They recruit, you mean. And if you're not interested in being recruited they 'transfer you.' To where? Out here, in the Desolation. Because, as you might have guessed, that's where you are. Ha. I see your fear. No worries. The stories of rads are exaggerated. You can die out here, sure, but not from standing around. At least, not from catching rads while standing around, anyway. Come on. I'll show you."

The two nameless men, whom Jackson seemed to have no inclination to introduce, tied Michael's hands behind him and took him back outside. Now that his head had cleared, the landscape looked less dreamlike and daunting and more just empty. He got his first good look at the cart he'd arrived in. He'd never seen anything like it.

The rear was something out of ancient times. The back wheels were huge with wooden spokes and some kind of metal wrapped around the rims. The rest of the cart was also rough wood with paint that had faded into a reddish brown where it still clung to the wood at all. The front was some sort of engine, open to the sky in a metal container with two flat, brown seats sticking up behind it. The front wheels were all metal and about half the size of the back wheels.

Jackson dragged a couple of plastic chairs over to the cart and threw them in the back.

"Our guest will sit back there with me. You drive, Justin."

So the mean man was called Justin. Justin hopped up into one of the front seats and began manipulating a series of shafts that led down into the engine. As he did so, the engine began to make some growling noises that were not loud but disconcerting, as if the machine was straining against itself. The other man tied Michael to a chair.

The cart ride took them down a slope away from the metal shack. The terrain barely changed. The same light dusting of green mixed in with dead, yellow vegetation in a grey soil.

Michael began to feel very sick. Was it the rads or the trip? He'd never been out of the Citadel. He'd grown up in the Complex, never away from the protective influence of the Authority. He felt himself begin to cry. There was nowhere to hide, strapped as he was into a plastic chair that moved and shuttered with every bump. He feared falling over or even out of the cart. At the same time, he wondered if he should jump. They hadn't tied his legs. What if he launched himself from the cart? Would it kill him? He almost hoped it would. He realized he couldn't run, even if he did jump. There was nowhere to go.

Tears welled up in Michael's eyes, slid down and clung to his cheeks. No wind blew to dry them. Jackson took no notice. Without Michael realizing they had even been climbing a hill, the cart crested the top. The landscape below was entirely alien. The cart trundled down a small path among what looked like snakes of metal winding in and out of each other across the ground in random patterns.

"The Plum Forest, we call it," said Jackson, speaking for the first time since they left the shack. "It's what's left of all the houses that used to stand here, or so they say. Heretics used to hide out here, so the Authority wiped them out with a bomb that burned everything but the pipes from the houses. At least that's one story. The other way I hear it sometimes is the Heretics suspected the people of overreliance on technology, so they burned them out. Either way, all you have left is pipe. One of the seven wonders of the wilderness I'm going to show you, Monk."

Michael could see it now. He knew very little about plumbing except that they had it in all the buildings in the New York Citadel. But how could so much be burned away without melting or destroying the pipes? Here and there, he noticed shreds of material clinging to the metal but nothing recognizable. The trip through the valley of metal seemed to take forever. Once, he was almost certain he saw a children's toy in the middle of one nest of pipes. As they got closer, he realized what he thought was a toy must be bones. But then, as they got closer still, it looked more like the pieces of a broken toilet bowl.

"I see you've spied the porcelain miracle," Jackson barked with a laugh. "Or what's left of it. Lots of us outcasts think it's a holy relic, like some you have back in New York. Although this one's quite a bit less useful than yours." Jackson eyed Michael when he said this. "But that doesn't stop some folks from stealing bits of it now and then. So the scraps are all that's left of the second wonder of the wilderness. Nobody knows why one porcelain toilet would survive here. You wanna know what I think?"

Jackson leaned in close to Michael so the Monk couldn't avoid the smell of the somewhat unhygienic man. "I think somebody brought it here later as a joke." Jackson whispered, then leaned back. "Some joke, huh?!" he shouted. "Get on up the hill, Justin! Let's show him the Crystal Palace!"

Justin worked the levers, and the cart picked up speed. They turned off from the main pathway and climbed a small rise where the plumbing thinned out. Over the top of this small hill was a riotous collection of fused glass. It looked like someone had taken hundreds of window panes, mirrors and any other glass they could get hold of, thrown it in a pile and then partially melted it. Shards of glass stuck out in sharp angles in many places, while streams of smooth, melted material flowed around the sharp points.

"What is it?" Michael couldn't help asking.

"Nobody knows," Jackson grunted, almost in disgust. "Every theory is different about the third wonder. Some say it was a refuse pile that got torched when the bomb went off. Seems likely. Others say it was some kind of Citadelian tech that went wrong and melted itself. Others think it was a space vehicle—maybe Moon men trying to get home—that crashed. You know what I call it?"

Michael didn't play along, but Jackson acted like he had anyway.

"A waste of time, old son!" Jackson cackled and clapped Michael hard on the back, almost making him vomit. Michael felt miserable now. It was the worst he had ever felt, physically and emotionally. He wanted it to end. He wanted to throw himself on the jagged spikes of the third wonder. He was manic but frightened to death of moving. He wished for death and salvation with every alternating breath.

"Cheer up, Monk!" Jackson said, oddly echoing Michael's state. "You won't die of this. You won't likely die of anything out here. Just enjoy the tour. Here comes the fourth." Jackson pointed up in the sky. Just in front of them, thick, black ropes bundled together and covered in bird droppings, hung between two immense metal towers. They were the tallest structures the Monk had seen outside of the Complex in Manhattan.

"No idea what this is either. Probably some kind of power or communication system from the Citadelian days. Certainly dates from then, anyway, whatever it was. Again, no idea how it survived or why. Probably just dumb luck. That's how WE done it, eh Justin, eh Bob?!" Jackson now clapped the two men as hard as or harder than he had clapped Michael.

So the other man was named Bob. Neither of the men turned to acknowledge the thought. Justin just fiddled constantly with levers and kept the cart moving forward.

"The fifth wonder of the wilderness is my favorite. Right down in this hollow. Some people don't even notice it. Do you see it?" Jackson asked.

Michael saw it. "Oh yes." At the bottom of the little hollow stood a tall, majestic tree. Not the kind nurtured on rooftops in the Complex. Not the scrubby mutants of the countryside in Queenlyn. A tree out of a storybook, tall and filled with leaves. It was twice, maybe three times, as tall as Michael. He had never seen anything like it.

Nothing but dead or half-dead scrub surrounded it, but somehow the tree had maintained its stature. As they got close, Michael saw that the tree looked sicker than it first appeared. The leaves hung limp. None were perfect and without holes. Insects crawled on the tree in too great a number to be beneficial. And the bark had a dry, dying look.

"Is it dying?" he asked Jackson.

"If it is, it's been doing so since before I was born. Enit boot," Jackson rasped, almost whispering, in the lingo of the Free Citizens. It was the first time he had lapsed into the slang. "Jussit boot, yeah." Jackson jumped off the cart and walked over to kneel by the tree. Michael wondered what he was expected to do.

"Just sit," Justin grunted at him. So Michael just sat. He couldn't do much else.

Jackson spent quite a long time by the tree. Michael took the opportunity to get his bearings. Or at least he tried to. Other than the sun setting in the west, he didn't really know enough to help himself. He ended up staring at the tree. Finally, Jackson returned.

"On to the sixth, Justin. The singing sixth! You'll get to come down off that chair for this one, Michael. Won't that be a treat?!"

It took awhile to get there, and nobody talked on the way. Eventually, they came up to a shack similar to Jackson's, made mostly of plastic but with a metal door. In fact, it was somewhat the opposite of Jackson's, Michael noticed. A homemade sign sat out front on the ground with the words, "Bar Open."

"Well, let's grab a drink," Jackson said.

They didn't untie Michael's hands, so he assumed he wouldn't benefit from these proposed drinks. Of the half-dozen people inside, nobody seemed to be surprised at a man in bondage.

There was no real bar. A man at a low table with benches attached to the sides of it served drinks into unmatched cups of various materials. A wild variety of chairs and small tables sat about the room, half of them occupied. A couple of people nodded or greeted Jackson, but none seemed overly friendly. Nor did the mean men engage with anyone, though all three got drinks.

In one corner of the room, which Michael now noticed was three or four times the size of Jackson's metal shack, stood an odd glass machine that looked incredibly fragile. Michael couldn't be sure, but he thought it glowed with a faint light.

Jackson approached it, a snake of a smile spreading across his face.

A slightly built bald man with a scar instead of a left ear, stood up and slurred, "Whudda finking of, Jackson?"

"Playn tunes uh my guest 'ere," Jackson waved toward Michael.

Jackson's confidence seemed to suck away some of the bald man's. "You makka yerselph purty free widdit, Jackson. You knows twont longy. Whya get take alla tunes?" The bald man spoke slang in a fighting tone mixed with petulance in an ugly, unflattering and entirely unpredictable way.

Jackson turned, the smile fading from his face, and spoke in proper language. "Let me explain real slow for you, Sammy." Faster than Michael could follow, Jackson slugged the bald man who fell unconscious to the ground. Michael felt nauseated again. He'd never seen anyone knocked out before. At least he hoped the bald man was only knocked out.

Jackson turned back to the glass machine and yelled, "Any quests?"

A somewhat surly silence answered him until a young voice—Michael couldn't be sure if it was female or male—yelled, "Over, over, over!" Michael didn't see who shouted it, but Jackson didn't turn.

"Y'goddit," he muttered. He pressed some buttons and music began playing.

Michael wasn't unfamiliar with recorded music. They used it in several of the rites and services in the Complex. But he didn't expect a machine sophisticated enough to replicate music would exist out here.

"A candy-colored clown they call the sandman…" a voice began to sing.

Jackson sauntered over to Michael who just stared.

"It's some kind of battery device. Plays music. An infinite amount of music from all eras, all styles—anything you can think of and even more that you can't. Nothing from recent times, of course, but then who wants that crap?

"Thing is like that—there's a battery life thing on it. Goes down a couple points every time you play a song. Nobody's figured out how to recharge it, so it will eventually die out. Folks in the bar all have to approve of you playing stuff before you can do it. I'm preapproved, you might say. Every so often, I get challenged from somebody like Sammy, drunk on the juice. Oh hell, it's usually Sammy. He does love that juice. I'd give you a glass but you need a little building up to it. I don't want you pass out for the last wonder, now do I?"

He slammed back his "juice," slammed the cup down and slapped his palm on the tabletop.

"Come on!" he motioned to the mean men, and they headed out the door.

"Whera toddle, Jackson? Ya jes madddit in? Ya song int ven done?" Michael recognized the voice that made the request. It belonged to a young, thin redhead who came running up to Jackson like a puppy dog.

"Gotta run, Pat, love. Alla back for long, ne worry."

The next wonder took quite awhile to get to. It was dark by the time they arrived. Jackson said it wouldn't matter. The cart pulled up outside a low wooden building with a curved roof. Torch fires burned outside, and men with guns guarded the door.

Michael expected to be challenged but the gunmen just waved them all through. Inside, a dozen or so people waited behind a crude hemp rope. At the other end of the wooden hall, an old man with grey hair and an old-fashioned suit of clothing stood by a screen, explaining something.

Jackson skipped the line and walked right up to the old man, who just kept talking.

"So we don't really know what that means," the old man was saying. "But it's not a bad sign, in any case."

Jackson remained uncharacteristically patient. When the old man was finished, he turned toward Jackson.

"Mr. Jackson. What trouble have you dragged into my observatory today?"

Jackson snickered and answered in slang. "Whatcha care boss, slong zit charge a baytree, ne?" Both men chuckled at this. The old man offered a hand to Michael then noticed the tied hands and withdrew it slowly.

"I'm Professor Panko," he said. "Sorry about the bonds, but it's probably for the best. I'm considered something of a Heretic, you see, so you might be required to kill me by your order or something." He chuckled to himself at this.

Michael's eyes grew a little wide in spite of himself. Had the man just admitted Heresy to a Monk of the order? What exactly was a professor? Was that slang? It sounded like "confessor." Was that what just happened? Had he confessed to Michael?

"Honestly, I don't hold with any of that Heretic nonsense about lack of freedom and progress, and I have no quarrel with the Authority as long as they keep the power on. But that's the issue. They don't. And they don't seem to like me complaining about it, or the fact that I seem to want to deal in facts about the Moon."

"The Moon?" Michael asked with true curiosity.

"Yes. Yes, the Moon. That's what I do. Jackson here calls me the seventh wonder of the wilderness, stupidly high praise for a man who simply kept his family's telescope in working order. He helps me scrounge batteries, and in turn I help him with odds and ends he needs. Nothing worth mentioning of course, right Jackson?"

"Trifles all," Jackson said with a wide smile.

"But come. You're not here for that. You're here to see this," he motioned toward the screen behind him and led Michael up to it.

On the screen were charts and flickering numbers and, in the middle, a light flicker surrounded by silver and shadows.

"This won't make any sense out of context. I'll give you a private demonstration."

Panko worked a keyboard and the image zoomed out to show the Moon. He slowly zoomed in while explaining.

"I've centered the image on the most likely location of the ancient Armstrong Station, or Citadel 32. As far as we know, the last contact with Armstrong was just before the Fall. They were technically self-sufficient and working out plans for an extended stay, though probably not as extended as it's turned out.

"So the question has been, 'Are they still there, or has the harsh, airless climate of the Moon gotten them?'"

That was the old man's first heresy, thought Michael. The Moon was not airless, according to the Authority; the air was just thin, like at the top of a mountain. But it wasn't a mortal heresy, so Michael kept it to himself and just listened.

"As we zoom in, you can start to see a dark spot where the Armstrong Station Dome is. There are also these very tiny dots where tunnels run out. And the one I've been focusing on is this tunnel here.

"Just in the last few days, I've noticed what I could swear is some sort of activity—and a light or at least a reflection. It looks to me as if something has been uncovered, and either they're shining a light on it, or it's reflective."

The image returned to its original dark landscape with a light spot in the middle. Now that Michael had a better idea of what he was looking at, he thought he could see the objects.

"What do you make of it, Michael?" Professor Panko asked.

"That looks like machinery of some kind, and these are tracks maybe? Possibly a car? I've heard they had some there. And this egg shape is very familiar. There's a Sculpture quite like it in the Reliquary." He stopped himself. Why was he telling this stranger all this? He wouldn't have told his fellow Monks this much. But he was excited. He was looking at the Moon! The more he looked, the more he was convinced the egg shape on the Moon was identical to the Sculpture in the Reliquary. Was this the Armstrong machine he'd been preparing to signal? If so, how did this wilderness Heretic have the tools to see it and not the Authority?

"Ah-ha!" Panko exclaimed. "They do have it. And if I'm right, that is the transmission machine. Oh, you've been very helpful, Michael. Very worth all the trouble. A pleasure to meet you. I'm only sorry that circumstances prevent us from truly working together.

Maybe someday eh, maybe someday? But not today. Thank you, Jackson. I was right, wasn't I?"

Jackson seemed to good-naturedly—but reluctantly—nod his head. "I should never doubt you, Professor. Come along, Michael."

As they left, Michael heard the old man excitedly tell the next person in line about his new discoveries and how they confirmed the Moon's inhabitants must have survived and likely held invaluable information.

"I showed you the Moon, Michael," Jackson said in an odd voice and accent as they climbed back into the cart. "Now let's see the stars!"

They rode most of the night. Michael drifted in and out of sleep as much as he could while tied to a plastic chair. Eventually, he woke from another nap to find they'd stopped. Moonlight showed enough of the road and surrounding landscape that Michael could tell they were at the edge of a cliff.

They pulled him down out of the cart again and walked him to the edge. In his dreamlike fugue of exhaustion and fear, he both worried and wished they'd throw him over.

"Look up and look down," Jackson said. Michael obeyed, too beat to resist. He looked up and saw the swirling stars of the sky, seemingly slightly more numerous than they looked near the Citadel.

Then he looked down and gasped. The stars existed on the ground below, more numerous than the stars above. It couldn't be reflection. It wasn't the same pattern of stars he was used to. Was it another universe?

Jackson stayed silent, letting him stare at the marvel. Finally, Michael asked the question. "What is it?"

Nobody knows. Some old technology that outlived its purpose but not its battery, I'm guessing. You can walk down in them too, and not discover anything more than lights in the ground. You can't dig them up and you can't break them. They shine all day and all night. Some people have dug tunnels underneath, but they can't find much of anything below them, either—a few legacy tunnels, probably left from when they were put in. But nobody can touch them. They're invulnerable. And their purpose is lost in time. Unless—"

After Jackson failed to finish the sentence, Michael asked, "Unless what?"

"Unless those men on the Moon know the answer," said Jackson. "But that's enough for tonight." He turned, suddenly and unexpectedly gruff. Let's pack it in and head back home. We'll have a talk tomorrow, Michael."

Michael slept most of the way back to the metal shack. He was dozing and dreaming about a sunny day in the courtyard of the Complex. While he spent most of his time hidden inside the Citadel, he only did so because of his anxiety around others. He longed for the sun and enjoyed the few times he felt comfortable outside lounging alone. Not that he got much time for lounging.

He woke to shouting. More men than Michael could count rushed up to the cart, grabbed the mean men and Jackson and carried them away. Two of the attackers grabbed Michael roughly and pulled him down as well, ripping his clothes and scraping his legs as they dragged him away from the cart like a sack. He could see the metal shack nearby, but the attackers were taking him in the other direction.

A nasty voice spit as it whispered uncomfortably in Michael's ear. "Shoutta want ye, Monk. Wedon care. A sooner ye tellat we need, a better."

With that, someone cracked Michael on the head and he heard, "Whajoo dodat for?" as he passed out.

CHAPTER 9

A lone man walked across a desert scene, his photon gun drawn. He wore a white shirt with a black vest and black pants.

An accented voice yelled, "Hey! Han Solo! Think fast!"

A bolt of fire kicked up dust in front of the lone man, who immediately squatted and returned fire. Suddenly, an implausibly large spaceship rose up above the horizon behind the lone man.

"I told you a million times, Duresh. I was headed to a Halloween party!" said the lone man.

The scene cut to a man standing in the same desert, wrapped in ungainly brown garments with a look of surprise on his face as he dropped his weapon and sank to his knees.

A mechanical-sounding voice spoke out of nowhere, ostensibly from the spaceship's speakers. "We can still make the party if we leave now, sir— and break a few hyperdrive laws."

"All right, Trinket. Let's roll. Just make sure Duresh here won't bother anyone else, OK?"

A red beam of light shot through the air from the ship. The scene cut to Duresh shaking his hand, his weapon a melted mess at his feet.

The lone man ran back toward the ship as the camera zoomed out. until you could only make out the spaceship, then the planet, and then you zoomed faster through a stellar system, then a galaxy, then a star field.

Credits began to roll. "So what did you think?" Corge asked LeAnn.

"Fine."

"Fine?"

"Fine."

"One of the greatest science fiction movies of all time, and you say, 'Fine'?"

"It was boring."

"How can you say THAT was boring? That is one of the greatest space battle sequences in movie history ever."

"Things don't explode like that in a vacuum."

"You're missing the point, LeAnn," Corge sighed.

"Oh, am I? And what is this essential point I'm missing? That everyone must like what you like?"

"What?!" Corge screeched. "EVERYBODY likes this movie. It has been consistently rated in the top five science fiction movies since before Disconnection!"

"Maybe that's why it's boring?"

Corge stared at her.

"It's old," she shrugged.

Corge took a deep breath to calm himself before mounting another defense when the station alert rang on his com.

"Yellow," LeAnn said. Corge stared at her, his eyes blazing coals of offense. "The alert, dummy. It's yellow. Might be interesting."

"Oh," Corge launched the alert. Its text replaced the movie credits on the screen.

"In an urgent session of Assembly, a Vote of Caution was taken on segmented matters. Teams A, 10, B, 75, HAB, 32 and 16B should consult team leaders for altered instructions."

"What the hell was that?" LeAnn asked Corge.

"A Vote of Caution means a passed measure received enough concern from committee experts to require a delay in implementation while more information is collected. It's a safety valve against measures that might have been honestly passed before previously unknown evidence could bear on the issue."

"Thank you, Mr. Textbook. I knew that. I mean, what's it about? Why is it segmented? It's not vent related, I know that much."

"Only one secret session I've been to lately. My guess is the Passives got a delay on the machine preparations."

"Oh crap," LeAnn sighed.

Corge's com rang again. LeAnn's rang at the same time.

"Meeting with Ibrahima?"

"Yep," Corge said. "All right, LeAnn. Let's roll."

LeAnn rolled her eyes. "Please tell me you're not going to quote that movie for the next week."

"No time to talk, LeAnn. We can make it to Ibrahima's if we leave now—and break a few hyperdrive laws."

"That isn't even the quote," LeAnn sighed.

"So you were paying attention," Corge smiled.

LeAnn hit him gently on the back of the head.

They met in Ibrahima's lab with Chi-lin and several other team members. Once they were all settled, Ibrahima spoke.

"As you may have surmised from the alert, the Passives organized a Vote of Caution on the work we've been doing to prepare for the machine. They took the vote without my knowledge, input or presence. That is not acceptable, but it is done.

"They found some psychological studies in deep databanks that they claim bear on the effect the machine work would have on the populous. They swayed the council by arguing this was not a veto of the Assembly's decision but a 'go slow' until the procedure could be adapted.

"To me, it's obviously the first step on the way to killing the project. Otherwise, why shut me out of the proceedings? In any case, we're awaiting new instructions from the Assembly. I'm told Serafina will arrive shortly with those.

"At best, we'll be told to limit our preparations to the point of transmission and not beyond. In that case, we carry on as usual and I'll only ask you for more speed. It will become a race to see if we can force a vote on transmission before they make their next move to shut us down.

"At worst, they convince the council to suspend our entire operation until the caution is lifted. In that case, you'll all find offers to assist me with my next, entirely unrelated project that is too early in its development to require me to inform the Assembly." She uncharacteristically winked. "Now, talk amongst yourselves while we wait. I have some messages to attend to." She sat down at her screen and ignored us all.

It didn't take long. Serafina shuffled in, carrying several info devices. The room quieted again, and she read from one of them.

"As I told Ibrahima, the Assembly was presented with new evidence of psychological studies to be weighed and incorporated into procedures for the machine reactivation sequence, thus instigating a Vote of Caution, which passed. I'd like to emphasize that your team is not being disbanded, and you still must operate under a strict nondisclosure policy."

A sigh of relief swept through the group.

"However, the limits of your immediate mission have changed. Transmission and Operation have been reclassified as follow-on missions. In accordance with the research needs of the Caution Vote, all efforts should be redirected into research internally. While survey missions on the surface are still authorized, the machine itself is off limits until further notice."

A groan swept through the group, driving out the relief.

"The Assembly has expressly restricted the machine to Assembly-specific authorizations only. Those authorizations are limited for the time being to Psychology team members on the new Effects Evaluation and Research mission. Thank you for your continuing work in this effort."

Serafina did not use any of the soaring tones or rhetorical devices she had displayed in the Assembly meeting. She kept a flat, emotionless voice through the entire reading. Now that it was done, she looked up and regret crept into her face.

"I'm really sorry, as I've told Ibrahima. None of us were expecting this Caution Vote. Some even suspect the Passives may have withheld evidence in initial discovery so they could spring this on us in case they lost the first vote. I doubt that. My guess is they got lucky with a random hit by one of their researchers and went with it."

"Why is the machine restricted?" yelled one of the team members.

Serafina just shook her head. "I'm not even sure. An argument was made that, to prevent accidental transmission, the team should be kept off the machine. Then Psychology noted they needed access, and somehow or another it ended up making sense to carve out a narrow exception for Psychology. When we tried to make a similar exception for specific Communication team members, it failed. We just didn't have the votes. Apparently the Passives have convinced several members of the Assembly that our—I mean your—team is too enthusiastic."

Ibrahima stood. "Thanks, Serafina. I know it's not what you wanted to hear, but at least the team is still together and we, in part, have Serafina to thank for that. We'll abide by the decision."

"Thank you, Specialist Ibrahima," Serafina said, then lowered her head and left.

Ibrahima waited until Serafina was gone and said, at full volume, "Like hell! I'll be damned if the Passives keep our hands off that machine. Keep planning as if we'll have access. Don't doubt it for a moment. We will find a way. Corge, Chi-lin, LeAnn, with me."

She called them over to her desk and began lecturing them in a low voice. Most of it was about the importance of the mission and how she was almost certain that the Caution Vote was illegal, and she said she'd even risk a trial to prove it.

"But I won't put you three in that position unless you agree. Back out any time, including now. Otherwise, I have a special task for you."

Her searing gaze told a different story than her words. Corge felt she might capture and torture any one of them who backed out. Or at least scorch them with her disapproving glare.

"Good. I need someone who knows the surface," she pointed at Chi-lin. "Someone who knows the tunnels," she indicated LeAnn. "And someone who knows the machine," she pointed at Corge. You're going to need to look like you're working in this lab every day and show that work to the Passives from the Assembly, but be ready to access that machine on my notice, get to it fast, and work it as if you'd been at the real thing every day. I can help you with the hiding—"

"I can't do it," Chi-lin said, interrupting her.

"What do you mean you can't do it," Ibrahima snapped, belying her assurance that they could walk away at any time.

"I want to," she said defensively, "I really mean I can't. I'm not capable. I'll get caught."

"What a pile of reclamation sludge. You will not," Ibrahima barked.

"Look at my record," Chi-lin protested. "I'm practically a Tripathi!" Even Ibrahima looked shocked by the self-insult. "I'm brilliant for part of any job, I know that. But I'm never good at all of it. I'm not reliable! This is too important to risk it on me." She ended this with a pleading look to Ibrahima.

"Insult yourself all you want, but don't insult me," Ibrahima said in an even tone. "Do you think I'm an idiot?"

"What? No! Of course not."

"Or do you think I'm growing feeble in my old age? That I'm no longer capable of judging risks or character?"

Chi-lin saw her point immediately and looked down.

"I'm not putting you in this job because I have some altruistic chance to do good by someone. You're right about that. I wouldn't risk this effort's chances of success to make you feel better. Stop flattering yourself. I don't think—I know—that you are the best for this job. You know the surface. You've been out there constantly. And you proved your ability to judge the terrain when you recovered from that ridiculous mistake you made up there at the machine.

"I'm pretty much counting on you to make some dumb error like that again. Partly because I know you're clever enough to recover from it and partly because it will be unexpected and something these prigs from the Passives won't anticipate. Be original. Be clever. Make mistakes. Just make damned sure you recover from them. Got it?"

The color drained from Chi-lin's face. "Yes, ma'am."

"Good. That's enough on that. Corge, the first phase depends on you. Remember, I said it's a race. The faster you figure out the machine, the faster we can make a break and try it. I need you to be five nines sure you can make it work, and I need you to get there fast. So get to work."

Corge just nodded.

"LeAnn, come with me. Your part will be easy since we just need to map out a few alternate routes out there. It'll be the easiest thing to hide."

Corge asked, "How do I hide my research?"

"Look in the files for 'Semiological Resonance Estimates.' It's the most boring title I could think of. Everything you need will be in there. Just open up stuff until you figure out what's what. Should be self-explanatory."

"What should I do in the meantime?" asked Chi-lin.

"Go up on the surface. You heard them. We can get to observational distance. Go scout some stuff out. Mess up some minor stuff. It'll lower their suspicions of you."

"Right," Chi-lin looked a little miffed by this. "I'll go do what I do best."

CAPITULUM 5

Michael woke to find himself tied to another chair. This one was all metal with spindly legs and a solid back. He had seen more types of chairs in the last 48 hours than he'd ever seen in his life. He began to giggle. He suspected he must be drugged and giggled again.

He opened his eyes and saw something that made him guffaw like a maniac while crying like a baby.

Jackson lay face up in a pool of blood at Michael's feet. His throat had been slit and they laid him spread eagle, a horrible rictus grin on his face, his eyes staring up into nothing. Michael heard his own uproarious laughter and began to vomit.

In his brief moments of clarity, Michael noticed the room. It was dark and there was a dim light coming from somewhere unidentifiable. He had no real sense of time. Waves of fear, panic, elation and delusion racked him in random order. All the while his only company was the dead body of Jackson and figments of his mind.

At some point, he fell unconscious. He woke to a man sitting on a stool in the place where Jackson's body had been.

"Feel better, Michael?" the man said.

The man wore a thick, grey shirt that Michael had heard called a "jumper" by some. It was always too hot in New York to wear such a thing. The man held a large knife in one hand, playing with it like a toy, rubbing its handles, cleaning his nails, poking the stool. Throughout their conversation, he kept the blade moving, but never in a menacing way.

"The drugs were meant to make you easier to transport, but uh—heh heh—they do have other side effects. Some even find them pleasant. From the way you look, I suspect you didn't," the man said.

Michael stared. The man had grey, rheumy eyes, short grey hair and a face full of wrinkles. He never smiled, but everything he said sounded like it carried a smirk.

"Why did you kill Jackson?" Michael rasped. His mouth was dry and his throat hurt.

"Get him some water," the man turned and shouted to someone Michael couldn't see, then turned back. "I'm not sure who Jackson is, Michael. But if you're meaning the men who held you before, we didn't kill any of them. I'm certain they'd like to kill us now, but we got you and were gone. We hurt them, sure, but nothing deadly—at least, that I'm aware of."

"You're lying. Jackson was dead right there on the ground in front of me," Michael countered.

"Here?" the man shook his head. "That's the drugs, Michael. I'm sorry that's what you thought you saw. It must have been horrifying. But you can see, nobody's been here. This is a dirt floor. It'd be awful hard to clean the stain up, or the smell for that matter. You see?"

Michael shook his head. "It's gravel. You could clean it."

The man sighed. "Well fine, Michael. I don't care if you think we killed your former captors or not. It doesn't much make a difference. So let's drop it before we get off to a bad start. I'm Martin Chao. I head a secret organization here in the wilderness that is the arm of a—well—let's calls it a faction of the Authority. It's hard to explain, but there are many factions in the Authority. Your Guteerez is part of one. My superiors are of a different faction."

"Dabashi's faction?" Michael asked.

The man shook his head. "No, but I can see why you might think so. From what I know, Dabashi's been giving you a hard time. But Dabashi doesn't have a faction. Or at least not one we know of. It makes him an oddity and quite interesting. He's been able to balance a very precarious neutrality. Not many people can manage that."

"What do you want with me?"

"Believe it or not, we didn't want you at all at first. We were willing to let you work on the machine, and then we planned to approach you directly at the Complex. But Guteerez's people moved before that. Maybe they thought all the factions would try to capture you. I don't think most would have, but Guteerez's faction captured you and took you out to that metal shack."

"Why would Guteerez do that?"

"I didn't say he did," the man raised his eyebrows. "In fact I'd bet he's a bit miffed that his faction did it. It seemed to me, his plan was to stay close to you until you were ready for transmission and stop any other faction from getting to you. But his betters had different ideas."

"So you want me to believe this was a rescue? Why am I here and not back at the Complex?"

"It's not safe," the man raised his eyebrows again. "If we took you back there, chances are you'd just get captured again. No, we had to keep you safe. We want what you want, Michael—the transmission codes for the Moon. We want to contact the Moon again. That is what you were working on, right?"

Michael started to answer, but his drug-addled brain presented him with a question he might not normally have asked himself. His habits were broken. He didn't automatically give the authority figure what it asked for. Why would the man who knew so much about factions and who was doing what to whom have to ask what he was working on?

"No," Michael shook his head.

The man stopped fiddling with his knife for a full second, the first time he had stopped playing with it through the entire conversation.

"What do you mean 'no,' Michael? We know that's what you were working on."

"Then someone told you wrong," Michael heard himself say, and let out a little giggle. "You've obviously got the wrong guy. As far as I know, the Moon men are just legends. Maybe true, maybe not, but none of my concern."

"You disappoint me, Michael," Chao said, frowning. "If you weren't working on a transmission vector, what were you doing in your secret room in the Reliquary of the Citadel?"

Michael felt suddenly powerful. It was probably the remaining effects of the drugs, but it felt good. He saw the depths of the man's ignorance in that statement. Nobody called it the "Reliquary of the Citadel"; it was just the Reliquary. Michael had no idea what "transmission vector" meant, but it certainly wasn't a common phrase in any of his studies of the Sculpture.

He laughed a loud, confident laugh and told Chao, "I was studying a Sculpture, in a very not secret room on a very not secret project. It's art history, Mr. Chao, not fairy tale exploration. If Guteerez was part of your so-called faction, maybe you could have asked him and he would have explained it." He finished with a rolling, painful belly laugh that was, frankly, out of his control.

Chao slapped him across the face with the flat of the knife, drawing a bit of blood as the blade grazed his nose.

"While I'm a patient man," Chao hissed, "I will not be mocked. You were working on transmission, and you will tell us how to access the equipment and how to bypass any encryption on it. Do you understand?"

Michael sobered up a bit after the slap and thought perhaps he had overplayed his hand. He nodded slowly.

"I didn't hear a response. Do I need to slap you again, Michael?" Chao sneered.

"No," Michael rasped again. "I understand."

"Give him his water," Chao shouted. "We'll do this the other way later."

Two women approached with a ladle and bucket, forced his mouth open and poured brackish, metallic-tasting water down his throat.

"You shouldn't have done that," one of them whispered. "Now he doesn't like you." Then they were gone.

Michael passed in and out of consciousness. He felt compelled to stay awake, but each time he thought he had succeeded, he jerked forward from some nightmare or other. Once he dreamed Guteerez and a dead Jackson, animated and spraying blood, were chasing him. The blood stuck like some kind of glue and slowed him down as he tried to get away. In another dream, Dabashi sat on a high podium wearing a white wig and pounding some kind of hammer, yelling obscenities at Michael while the two mean men held him and forced his head up to listen. In another, Chao crept over Michael's body, sometimes like a bug, sometimes like a baby, sniffing in every hollow and crevice but never quite touching Michael. Each time he got to the point in the dream when he cried out, he would wake up yelling to nobody, still tied to the chair.

Eventually, Chao returned with his hands full of rusting metal tools. He stood in front of Michael, dropped the tools at his feet and gave him a level, uncaring look.

"So, Michael. I've brought these old tools as a contingency. Do you know what a contingency is?" He didn't pause for an answer. "A contingency is something you plan, but hope not to use. It only actually becomes the plan if your main plan fails. I do not want my main plan to fail. My tools are old, rusty and dull. They tear when they should cut. And I am out of practice. I make mistakes. I do not want to make mistakes on you, Michael. I do not want to use my contingency plan. Do you understand?" He finally paused.

Michael nodded though not in acquiescence. If asked at that moment what he would do next, he would not have been able to say. He nodded only to indicate that he understood what a contingency was and what Chao's rusty, tearing, metal tools could do to him if he did not cooperate. Michael did not nod to indicate he would cooperate.

"Good," Chao said and sat down on the empty stool. The tools were not in easy reach, still scattered on the ground where Chao had dropped them. That reassured Michael a bit.

"So this should be over quickly then, Michael," Chao grinned a smile that looked genuine to Michael. He truly believed that Chao had no intention or desire to use the tools. That Chao wanted only the best for Michael. Could the woman have been wrong? Did Chao still like Michael? Michael wondered if he should care if Chao liked him or not, then wondered what to do next. He was far from any life he ever knew or remembered. He was tired, hungry and still thirsty, even after the little water they gave him. He was too exhausted to feel frightened, though his body pumped the fluids of fear through him. Michael began to cry.

Chao made a sound like "Tsk tsk tsk." He stood up from the stool, walked over and laid a hand on Michael's shoulder. "I understand too, Michael. It has been hard for a Monk like you, so sheltered in the Complex. So used to a routine where everything is provided. You may not eat the best food, but you always eat. You may not sleep in the best bed, but you always sleep. This can be over now, my friend," he patted Michael on the shoulder and returned to his seat on the stool.

"Tell me how to access the machine. Just where it is and what controls it, nothing complicated. Give us the encryption codes we need to use it. Just be honest. Tell us what you can, Michael, and you'll return to the Complex to eat and sleep as you used to, safe in your own bed, among your colleagues."

The thought tantalized Michael. He wanted desperately to be back in familiar territory. But it had been a mistake for Chao to tell Michael about Guteerez, whether true or not. Michael no longer thought of the Complex as safe. He thought of dangers at every turn. He thought of Dabashi hating him. He thought of Guteerez plotting against him. He thought of other Superiors with hidden agendas. Whether Chao told the truth or not, there was no ignoring the fact that someone had captured Michael from within the Reliquary. Then someone else had stolen him away from his captors. Both wanted something from the Monk, and the only people who wanted something Michael had were the people of the Complex.

Chao tapped his feet. "You can take your time, Michael, but why string it out? Just tell us. Gather your thoughts, tell us and you will be safe."

Michael felt the pull of promised safety. Would it be safer to tell and return? Or would someone else capture him as soon as he got back? Would he really be returned?

"You want to kill me afterward, don't you?" he asked.

Chao scoffed. It seemed genuine. "No, Michael, I do not want to kill you. Ever. I only want the information I seek. You made this unpleasant with your attitude before, but I understand why you acted out. You're scared. You forgot your training. But now we can be pleasant. Now we can be Monks of the Citadel and speak plainly and be done with unpleasantness."

Chao showed his partial ignorance again. Michael was a Monk of the Citadel, but he was not trained in the disciplines Chao seemed to refer to. Those were fighting Monks of the defense guards, not Michael. Chao seemed to think all Monks were the same. Michael was convinced more than ever that Chao was a hired gun with limited contact and understanding of the Superiors and the Complex. Had he been hired to deliver Michael and the information or just the information?

"Take me back and I'll show you."

Chao chuckled. No, Michael, I don't think so. It doesn't work like that. Too many eyes are watching there. I can't just waltz into the Citadel and tell them I'm with you. I'm not the one that needs this information anyway. You know that. I'm just the one asked to get it from you. And I will," he bent down and picked up one of the metal tools off the floor and began to play with it the way he had played with the knife. "One way or another," he said, looking at the rusty pliers in his hand.

Michael felt something break inside him then reveal a core like strong iron. It was as if a soft shell had fallen off his soul, taking his vulnerability with it.

"Then get it," Michael said quietly without taking his eyes off Chao.

For a moment, he saw the old man waver. Then Chao let out a great sigh. "Oh, Michael. I'm too old for this." But he bent down anyway and began gathering the tools up and sticking them in loops on his belt, one by one. He left the pliers in his hand as he approached Michael. "But here goes," he sighed and then Michael watched the most unnerving grin he'd ever seen take shape on Chao's face. Michael's newfound iron core wavered but did not break.

CAPITULUM 6

Michael couldn't see. He didn't mind. He didn't want to see. He was living in the ebb and flow of pain. It was his only care. He had learned to separate himself from it when he could, but it didn't make it easier to bear. He still screamed inside his mind sometimes and probably out loud as well. He couldn't tell the difference anymore anyway. But he no longer felt a desperate urge to take action. He resigned himself to waiting and living through it and so preserved his self.

He knew either death would take him or the pain would recede a little. When it receded, he didn't feel relief, for it never entirely left. Instead, he felt a curtain fall between himself and his awareness, and he was able to form thoughts that didn't focus solely on pain.

In those moments of respite, he listlessly tried to remember what they wanted. Not that he could remember things or even form whole thoughts. He could barely remember the Reliquary. He could only think about the pain and things related to the pain.

A hoarse voice, Chao's voice, the only voice, whispered in his ear.

"I know what you think now, Michael, because you only can think of one thing. I have boiled you to your essence. Now rest. Let your mind heal. Let the pain recede. Then your mind will return cleansed and we can talk again."

Michael felt his lips forced apart and cool liquid poured down his throat. Pain flared in protest then receded as the water did its work. The veil between consciousness and unconsciousness was so thin, he honestly couldn't tell when he passed out.

When he woke, the pain was dull and distant. He felt drugged again but pleasantly so. His thoughts were muddled, but they were whole thoughts again. And he could see. The room around him was no better than before, but he could see it. And he could think about it. He could ponder its dirt floor. He could watch Chao walk in and sit on the stool, no tools in his belt this time. He could think of responses and once again feel his metal core. He imagined it as pitted and scarred but yet unbroken. He also could remember the encryption codes again and where the Sculpture was.

"So, Michael. I tire of this and, well, I know you tire of it too. You think I want to kill you but I don't," he stretched these last words out with a bitter expression and shook his head. "I do not want this for you or me. I read an old book once where one of the characters ripped his soul to gain some advantage. He kept ripping it and ripping it to become powerful, but his soul weakened. That's what I feel like. It rips my soul. I do not want to rip my soul anymore. I do not want to rip your flesh anymore.

"Let's start with the machine. How do we access it?"

"You will just kill me anyway," Michael responded, not knowing how he formed the words, not meaning to. He just heard them come out, straight from the core.

"Then," the old man looked genuinely disappointed and sad, "we continue until you realize the truth." He dragged his feet as he loped out of the room.

Michael stole a smile. Whether it was an act or not, seeing Chao defeated was better than any relief or drug. Michael felt like he had the upper hand. For now.

CHAPTER 10

Corge's ears rang for minutes every time they stopped the drill. For a secret plan, it was extremely loud.

"How much more do we have to go?" He yelled.

"You don't have to yell anymore," LeAnn said. "We turned off the drill."

"Tell my ears!" Corge yelled anyway.

"Well, if you wore your helmet, maybe it wouldn't bother you," LeAnn tapped the side of the helmet that covered her whole head.

Corge shrugged. "I can't hear you through your helmet!" he shouted.

LeAnn pulled her helmet off and threw it at him. "Put it on!" she threatened.

"Live a little," Corge said, and tossed it farther up the tunnel by the nonessential supplies where his own helmet lay.

"Why, you insubordinate piece of—ever since you gained star status I—"

"Can you hold off on the flirting for a moment? I have a question," Chi-lin interrupted, smirking. That stopped LeAnn in her tracks.

"We weren't—flirting. W-what is it?" she snapped, forgetting about her helmet for the moment.

Chi-lin consulted the map. "Looks like we have a few more clicks to go. LeAnn, are we still taking the right jog near the end, or are you doing a slow curve? I can't remember."

LeAnn sighed without subtlety. "I'm going to tattoo it on your arm. We curve. Even though it uses more energy now, it saves a lot when Corge has to bring his equipment through. Why he needs all that equipment in order to press a few buttons, you'll have to ask him. I thought this was going to be a mapping mission, not a drilling mission. Do you know how much trouble I can get in?"

Corge snapped, "Maybe I should tattoo how much trouble you'll get in on your hand."

LeAnn looked sorry. "Come on, Corge. I didn't mean anything." She reached out toward him but he stomped off through the middle of the huge powered-off driller's open-air center and into the smaller service way, which hadn't been drilled yet. He stooped under the drill's circular blades and stayed stopped. In front of the drill, the service way was too small to stand up in.

"See?! I can't even stand up in here," he pointed at his stooping self. "I don't need that much equipment, LeAnn, but I do need to be able to stand to carry it, OK? I'm not a robot that can bend down and carry on for hours!"

LeAnn had followed him and stooped next to him in front of the drill. She had continued to look sorry until he said this last when her expression changed.

"Oh, so I suppose I'm the robot, then. Is that it?" she asked. "I don't like your favorite—"

A loud crack interrupted them from above. She knew that sound. It filled her nightmares.

"RUN!" LeAnn yelled and turned back toward the drill, but it was too late. Rock had already started to rain down by the time they heard it. By the time she yelled "run," it was tumbling down all around them. Fortunately for both right then, and unfortunately for her at any other moment in her life, LeAnn had seen several tunnel collapses. She knew which way the rocks were falling.

If they ran the short distance back to the drill, they had a small chance of making it, but it was more likely that they would get crushed inside the drill. She could tell this was a big one. Running the other direction meant crouching down and fighting your instincts, but it would likely save their lives.

In the infinitesimal fraction of a second that her brain processed this knowledge and applied it to the pattern of falling rocks, Corge started to valiantly push her toward the drill. She shoved him the other way up.

"What are you doing?" He yelled, sounding as if he thought she was trying to kill him.

She didn't answer but pushed harder then squeezed past him and pulled. Her insistence got through to Corge. She knew tunnels, and he had to know she wouldn't risk his life.

The rocks beat on her back now. She felt as if she were being punched or beaten. She was—by Lunar rocks. Thankfully, the rocks didn't weigh much, but the number of them meant they still posed a threat.

The dust choked them. She realized this was a probably a good sign. If they were choking, it meant they were breathing and not exposed to vacuum. The deadliest part of tunnel collapses usually wasn't the falling rocks; it was loss of air pressure.

She dragged Corge by the hand, but the more rocks fell, the slower she went. The tunnel narrowed. She knew it wouldn't get wider. This tunnel narrowed to an arm's width at its end near the surface. She couldn't see anything through the dust. She couldn't quite breathe through it, either. Every patch of her body was sore. The rock falls slowed but still hit every few seconds. She and Corge bent into a crawl.

Finally, like waiting for a bag of puff pops in a microwave, the falling rocks slowed enough that it was safe to stop. Corge flopped down on the floor of the tunnel next to her. She could barely hear his breathing over her own.

The distant sound of falling rocks quieted and they could hear nothing else. She had no idea how far they'd gone. It felt like the whole thing had taken a long time, but she knew it couldn't have been more than a minute. Her breathing steadied. It looked like the air would hold for a little longer. Corge's breathing slowed as well and he gasped, "You win."

"What?" she managed to wheeze. "Win what?"

"The argument," he spluttered. "You didn't have to collapse the tunnel to do it, you know."

She laughed, which made it harder to catch her breath. Between gasps, she managed to say, "It—worked—didn't it?"

He started to giggle himself, "A little too well."

"That's not good," she said, giggling in spite of herself. "It's not that funny."

This brought Corge's laughter to a mild rumble. "Are we losing pressure?"

"I don't think so," LeAnn sniffed the air a bit. She knew how to smell for pressure, a chief talent of tunnel Specialists like her. "Must be some kind of gas leak, though I don't know where it would come from." She fought the urge to giggle. It wasn't funny. But her brain found everything humorous right then.

"Look at that pipe?" Corge almost shouted, stifling a guffaw.

An incredibly old metal pipe jutted out of the rock above them, broken by the cave-in.

"Is it hissing?" Corge couldn't help but smile and start to laugh at this joke. Except it wasn't a joke. It was death.

"Yeah!" LeAnn choked off the word. They had crawled up a small pile of rubble toward the pipe. Somewhere in her mind, LeAnn knew that unless they could cap it quickly, moving toward it was the wrong thing to do.

"Cap it," she squeaked, and Corge almost busted a gut laughing at this but at the same time desperately searched for something to plug the hole. Suddenly he started taking off his outer shirt.

"No time for that," she couldn't help but say, making him pause as he fought off his own mirth, shaking his head and pointing at the pipe.

"Water," was all he managed to say and pointed at the ground.

She got it. Stuff the shirt in the pipe, make some mud out of dust with water from their flasks, and fill the gaps with wet dust as a seal. Then hope there was enough air movement in the tunnel to dissipate the gas that already escaped.

It took several minutes to finally plug the hole, but it seemed to work. The hissing stopped. At one point, the shirt began to move and it looked like the pressure would foil their plan, but some more wet dust in the right places seemed to stabilize it.

"That should hold for now," LeAnn said. "Good idea."

"Observation," Corge said, and let out a satisfyingly unhappy "ha," that wasn't prompted by a lack of oxygen in his brain.

"I think the air cleared," LeAnn said.

"You're always telling me to wear a helmet," he said. "Why aren't you wearing a helmet?"

"You're a bad influence," LeAnn spat. "Do you think Chi-lin's all right?"

"I would think so. She was on the other side of the drill last I saw her and pretty far from it. She should have seen it coming, easy."

"I hope you're right," LeAnn sighed and stood up as much as she could in the narrow tunnel. She followed the pipe as far back as possible into the rock above them.

"N2O," she finally read off the pipe. "That would have been my guess."

"Why is there an N2O pipe way out here?" Corge asked.

"We're not that far, really," LeAnn said. "The refinery and main fuel engine is two clicks," she paused and moved her hand about as if she was dowsing. "That way," she said when she finally landed on a direction. "Probably some kind of fuel mixture thing. I bet it comes from Chemistry Ops. Byproduct of something or other, headed out here through the rock where it can't hurt anyone," she laughed but again it was a perfectly honest and somewhat miserable laugh.

Corge began to crawl back the way they came. He couldn't see far down the tunnel. Their headlamps had come on automatically during the cave-in but didn't penetrate far. He got a few steps away and hit a pile of rocks. They didn't entirely fill the tunnel.

"Think we can dig our way back?" he asked.

LeAnn looked thoughtful. "Maybe. If we feel any kind of vibration, we need to back off right away. If they come to find us, they won't use the widening drill, but they might use another kind. We don't want to lose a hand right before we get rescued."

Corge looked horrified. "I hadn't even thought of that. But I meant, is it possible to dig through all this?"

LeAnn nodded slowly. "Sure. At least it looks like it from here. We'll have to see what we run up against as we get nearer the main cave-in point. Plus we need to be careful not to cause another fall."

It was slow work, especially trying to figure out what to do with the rock and dust they moved out of the way. They didn't want to block the way back up the tunnel in case they needed to retreat again. Secondary cave-ins were atypical but certainly not impossible. Eventually, they couldn't keep enough room behind them and still remove rock from in front of them.

Corge sat down, exhausted. "I know it's probably just the hard work, but the air seems thinner here. That wouldn't make any sense, would it? We're headed back toward the source. It should be getting richer."

LeAnn breathed heavily, too. "I don't know. Maybe we're losing air from a crack in the tunnel." She shook her head. "We might want to investigate the tunnel near the surface," she shrugged.

Corge looked a little shocked. "Why? There's nothing that way but vacuum, right? I mean, can't we just take a little more time to spread out what we've dug and keep going here?"

LeAnn shook her head. "No. It's not going to help. I can tell. This cave-in is pretty solid. We haven't hit the concentration point yet. The material keeps getting denser. That means we haven't hit any of the main cave-in points yet, which means we're not yet halfway. Imagine having to do everything we've done, times at least two, and slower as we spread the material out farther up the tube."

Corge looked a little desperate. "OK. But what choice do we have? You're not giving up are you?"

"No, idiot." LeAnn scowled at him and punched him somewhat hard on the shoulder. "Yeah right, I've decided to just throw in the helmet and die. Which, by the way, I wish I had right now, you dumbass."

"Don't call me a dumbass," he said, trying to pretend not to be actually hurt. Corge realized just how stupid it was to act sensitive about insults at a time like this. "What's your plan?"

LeAnn looked a little sheepish. "Well, it's not so much a plan as it is a hope."

"What hope?"

"Telfer tubes."

"What tubes?"

"Telfer tubes."

"What the hell are Telfer tubes?"

"Some of the earliest ventilation hacks from right after Disconnection. Supposedly invented by a guy named Telfer."

"Oh. I've heard of him. He led the team that laid the foundation for the recycling and reuse system. Right. He was in charge of the ventilators. Never heard of Telfer tubes, though," said Corge.

"Of course not, because you're not a Specialist in vent, like me. Telfer's most famous for general quality assurance. That's what you remember learning about. But he did a lot of detailed work on the system of fluid and gas reclamation. One of his early hacks was to create a system that efficiently rerouted air and gas back where it was needed. He took advantage of natural air currents."

"OK," Corge said doubtfully. "How does that help us?"

"Well, it was the Disconnection right? A little bit of chaos was going on, so his hack tubes never got properly mapped. Plus, his system couldn't draw any power since generation wasn't very good yet. Eventually, they figured a more efficient powered system involving small tubes. When that happened, the Telfer tubes were abandoned. A lot of folks think we wouldn't have survived Disconnection without them. We came pretty close to running out of water and air a few times back then."

"Of course," Corge nodded. "Now that you mention it, I remember Telfer getting some of the credit for systems that got us through those crises, but I never learned exactly what he did. Figured it was just ventilation stuff."

"Well, that's why I'm a Specialist and you're a—whatever you are—a Watcher. I was very interested in what Telfer was doing and wrote an independent examination of it. That's where I learned about Telfer tubes. They still exist, and they're all over the place. They just act as sort of passive storage now. Not worth bothering with."

"But you said they'd never been mapped."

"Right, which means there might be one up ahead of us near the surface. They ran everywhere. Or I should say, anywhere is as likely to have them as anywhere else. It was a hack. If we can find one, we might be able to crawl through it to somewhere on the other side of the collapse."

"But you can't be sure one is up there. Even then you don't know where it would lead to."

"I told you, Corge—it's a hope, not a plan."

Corge began to get up into the stooped position they called "standing" in that part of the tunnel. "Well, let's go take a look, then."

CHAPTER 11

The air thickened as Corge and LeAnn climbed back over the rubble to the place where they had started digging. For the first time in a while, Corge felt like he could fully stand up.

"Do you feel that?" LeAnn asked him.

Corge wasn't sure what she meant. They were standing very close together but also in rather thick tunnel suits. "Feel what?" he asked.

"A breeze."

Corge stopped. He wasn't sure if it was the power of her suggestion or if he actually felt a breeze. "I think. Maybe. I feel something," He felt his face grow hot after he said this last.

"It's definitely a movement of air. Very slight. But it's coming from up ahead toward the surface, not back by the collapse."

"A Telfer tube?" Corge asked hopefully.

"Or a leak near the surface, sucking the last of our breathable air out and losing us a few more years off of max station survival," she said in her "just stating the facts" voice. Corge often hated her "just stating the facts" voice.

"So, hope or death, which is it to be?" he sighed.

"You're a lighthearted one," she chided.

They kept moving toward the surface and the vent tunnel got small enough that they couldn't even stoop. Corge felt the breeze on his cheek but still wasn't convinced he wasn't imagining it. Then he felt a brief gust. He was sure of it. An actual gust of somewhat stale air had blown past his face and rustled the whiskers on his cheek.

"Did you feel that?" LeAnn asked.

"Yes!" he squeaked. "I damn well did! That was a breeze. So I'm not imagining it."

"No, you're not," and they felt another one. "And here's why. Scoot up near me."

Corge got very close to LeAnn and put his head right below her neck. Her shoulders had blocked his view of another vent tunnel intersecting with this one. A small waft of air came out as he looked into it. He felt LeAnn put an arm around him as he stared.

"Problem is," she said, "it's wide enough farther in, but we can't fit through the entrance. We'll have to dig it out to get in."

Corge could see what she meant. It looked like he could stand up inside this new tunnel. But the entryway was barely as big as his head.

"Too bad I'm not a cat," he said.

"A cat?" She laughed. He felt the laugh through her whole body, as it was wrapped around him.

"Yeah. Supposedly they could fit into any opening they could get their head into."

"Hmm," LeAnn said and slid out from under him, wrapping her upper body more around him, putting her head right next to his so they could both see into the hole. "That gives me an idea."

CHAPTER 12

"And I'm in!" LeAnn shouted from inside the new tunnel.

"How in the hell did you do that?" Corge marveled.

"I'm a cat," she teased. "Come and get me."

"Not a chance," Corge laughed.

"No, really," she got serious. "You can do it. You just fold your shoulders. They have to go out of the socket a bit. Painful for an instant, but in that instant you're through and you pop them back in."

"I cannot do that," he said.

"I thought everyone could do that." LeAnn sounded mystified.

"I'm not that flexible."

"Oh really? Too bad," she teased.

"Plus I'm too big."

"What do you mean?" she had half a smile and half a frown on her face. She looked like she couldn't decide if he was joking or telling her some unfathomable thing.

"My head's bigger than the hole." And he plunked his head up so his face filled it.

"Oh," she said. "Too bad to be you," she laughed again. Then took off running up the Telfer tube.

"Hey!" Corge yelled. He was as jealous of her ability to run in that tube as he was of her being in it.

"Be right back," she shouted over her shoulder. "Just checking something."

Corge thought about what they were doing while he waited. Now that it had gone from sneaking around to trying to find a way back into the base, the whole fragility of their world hit home. Like everyone he knew, Corge was raised to consider the long-term effects of everything he did. It informed the smallest, most mundane acts. But it also faded into the background. While no one decision made by him or Ibrahima felt like it violated any of his core principles, he wondered if that was really true.

If they circumvented the rules of the Assembly, weren't they doing exactly what the Passives feared? The Assembly was one of many safety nets to keep civilization, or "survivalization" as some of his teachers called it, stable and long-lived. If Ibrahima succeeded, wouldn't that undermine the Assembly's authority? The problem wasn't that anyone would revolt now. The problem would come years later when someone pointed back at what Ibrahima did and used it to justify whatever action they wanted. That action might be good, or it might not be. Worse, it might be well intentioned but deadly, and the safety check of the Assembly wouldn't catch it.

Who were they, anyway, to move against the Assembly? The Passives weren't evil. They were just cautious. Their voice deserved to be heard more than any other. And it had been, Corge realized. In a fair vote, the Passives had lost and this very operation had been approved. It was the Passives who wanted to game the system. Nobody he'd spoken to felt the purported new evidence would really end up proving a danger. Of course he hadn't spoken to any Passives, but he had spoken to plenty of Moderates.

Ibrahima was right, and most people agreed. The Passives amplified the evidence to slow progress and moved to cancel the project. It wasn't a safety valve. It was an attempt to force a minority view. When he thought about it that way, Corge felt compelled to do what they were doing. It felt imperative to carry out what seemed to be the true will of the Assembly. He realized every great criminal in history probably felt the same, but that didn't change his opinion. What they were doing wasn't risky. It was right.

He heard LeAnn huffing and puffing, running back toward him in the Telfer tube.

"This tube is HUGE," she shouted before he could even see her. "I never knew Telfer tubes were so big, especially this near the surface. It must have been a major vent shaft conduit!" She was grinning from ear to ear. Vent mechanics really did get her blood going. Corge decided he should learn more about the subject.

"The what with the who?" he joked.

"Never mind," she shook her head, panting but still smiling.

"Is the air thinner in there?"

"No, I was sprinting. I went a lot farther than I meant to. There's lots of cool stuff in here. Some that might even be interesting to the vent-ignorant," she waved a hand toward Corge, still catching her breath.

Corge laughed. "OK. Did you figure out how to get us out of here? Or how to get me in there?"

"Oh yeah, no," she said quickly, nodding as her breathing slowed. "We'll just have to dig you in. May take a bit, but we've had lots of practice today, haven't we?"

"Is it even still today?" Corge wondered.

"How philosophical. Anyway, as to the major question of getting us out of here, yes and no. I found one definite way to get back into the station but it's in Docking Bay. At least, I think it is."

"Wow, you did go far!"

"I didn't go all the way there; I just recognized the vent."

"Amazing."

"Stop it. That's a very not secret way to get back in, but it's good to know. I think, with a little more exploration, we could probably get back to the other side of the cave-in. I even saw some networks that might give us a good alternate route to the machine."

"All right," Corge sighed and smiled at the same time. "Shall we start digging?"

CHAPTER 13

"No, it's a solid cave-in, Ibrahima" Chi-lin said over her com. "After we got the widener out, we found a wall of rubble. We hand dug a bit, but that would take forever. We didn't even get to the central collapse point. It's amazing we got the widener drill out at all. I'm sorry—we're going to have to call in rescue. We'll need a slow drill team to find them."

Ibrahima's tinny voice came out of Chi-lin's com. "And there's nothing else you can try? It's not just that I'm hesitant to reveal what we've been up to. Waiting for a rescue team burns up time, too. If they are hurt, they need the fastest response possible."

"Unless you have some ideas, we're fresh out. No alarms were set off?"

"No," Ibrahima said. "Which makes me worry about them more. If they were moving and giving off heat signals, it should have set off sensors."

"Maybe, maybe not," Chi-lin said hopefully. "We're pretty far up. If the cave-in didn't set off an automatic alarm, it means it's above the sensitivity grid and didn't impact airflow. So if they did make it out from under, they must have had enough air."

"We did," LeAnn said, almost out of breath from behind Chi-lin.

Chi-lin squealed and screamed and leaped and hugged LeAnn all at once.

Muffled under all the hugging, Corge could barely hear Ibrahima's tinny voice yelling, "What!? What happened? Whose voice was that?"

When they all settled back down, Chi-lin, barely able to form words through her grin said, "Well, I didn't kill them. LeAnn and Corge just walked up behind me. How in Schmitz did you guys find your way out of there? That tube has no other access but the surface." Chi-lin's eyes grew wide as she began to consider the idea of them walking in vacuum without suits.

"We're not supermen," Corge assured her. "LeAnn found an old Telfer tube."

"A Telfer tube? Up there?" Chi-lin asked. "I thought they were all small pipes down by Central."

"Well, at least you know what they are," LeAnn smirked and nudged Corge.

Ibrahima's voice crackled over the com. "It must have been a main bypass. They allegedly used those a lot right after Disconnection. In fact, there's a big argument over whether there really were big tubes near the surface or if we misread the records. Nobody's ever found one until now. It's a historical find in addition to a life-saving one."

"It also means you can stop worrying about clearing out this cave-in for now," answered LeAnn. "I'm 98 percent sure I found an alternate route to the machine, and one even less likely to be noticed."

"Now that IS a historical find," Ibrahima answered.

"Historical or not, we should get to it," Corge said, uncharacteristically impatient. "We lost a lot of time here. How much, actually?"

"About 12 hours," said Chi-lin. "You two need to sleep and eat first."

Corge shook his head but Ibrahima contradicted him, even though she couldn't see his response.

"Don't argue, Corge. I know you're worried about the Passives. Leave that to me. We'll keep them at bay for now. Get rested and fed and in six hours we'll go over your Telfer tube plan. Go!"

Chi-lin's com made the characteristic pop of a closed connection.

"You heard her," Chi-lin smiled. "I'll clear all this up and do my best to explain the cave-in."

CAPITULUM 7

"Miiii-chaellllll," a sing-song voice accompanied the flashing of a knife in front of his eyes. "You've slept long enough, Michael. Time to work the machine, Michael."

The knife moved away to reveal Guteerez. He was using the knife to peel potatoes. "I will make us these potatoes, Michael. Doesn't that sound good? I knooooow you're hungry. Just work the machine. Go ahead. I'll make the food." Guteerez waved his knife toward the control box.

Michael noticed that they were in Jackson's metal shack. But the machine was there. He couldn't quite see the control box behind one of the old tables in the shack. He looked around. The shack seemed bigger than before. When he looked back, the music machine from the bar blocked his way to the box.

"Don't mind that," Dabashi's voice came from behind the machine. "Just work the machine!"

When Michael walked around the music machine, he found the control box, but in the middle of it, where the screen and controls would be, sat Dabashi's head. Chao was removing part of Dabashi's skull.

"The controls were in there all the time, Michael. We just needed to open it," Chao smiled in a gentle way.

"Hurry up, Michael. Before I forget everything. It's these parts here," and Dabashi's eyes looked up toward his open brain. Somehow Michael knew what he meant. Parts of Dabashi's brain glowed. Michael had never seen brains before. They were red, pulsing lamps like light bulbs. Dabashi's brain was laid out in the same way as the control box.

"Is it OK for Chao to see?" Michael asked doubtfully.

"Yes, of course," said Guteerez from his chair across the room.

"It can't be helped," snapped Dabashi. "It needs to be done. Stop delaying."

"I'm here," Chao said, raising his palms up in a shrug. "What can you do?"

Suddenly, Jackson barged in the room and with unnatural speed shot Guteerez and then Dabashi's head, destroying the controls.

"That was a mistake," Chao said.

"No, it wasn't," Michael answered slowly. "I can still control it. Look, the brain is glowing. Look! Look!"

Michael snapped awake from his nightmare to see one of the women attendants. "You were dreaming," she said. "What were you yelling 'look' about?"

"Nothing," Michael croaked. The woman spooned him the usual ration of water and gruel.

"How long have I been here?" Michael asked.

"You know I'm not allowed to say. You ask me that three times a day, you know," she answered.

Michael thought maybe she was trying to help him, but he couldn't remember how many times he had asked her. He'd long ago lost track. Was it 12?

"How many times?" he gasped.

She smiled but then they both heard footsteps. She said no more and hurried out of the room.

Chao came in without speaking and got to work. Michael no longer expected talk. They all knew the question. He would not give the answer.

CHAPTER 14

"And you're sure this will hold vacuum seal?" Corge said, pointing to the big metal ball LeAnn had finished installing at the end of the Telfer tube.

"Yes, 1000 times, yes. I'm not planning to pull the plug on the balloon that is our civilization," she said, using a crusty old phrase, implying how much of an old worrywart he was being.

If what LeAnn said was true, Corge could suit up, walk into that metal ball, unseal the ancient Telfer tube's access to the surface, and be 10 meters from the machine.

It hadn't been easy getting there. LeAnn and a small team spent several days discovering more bewildering networks of Telfer tubes. It amounted to enough previously uncalculated air that, after this was all over, they could add a bit of time to Armstrong's longevity clock.

After many dead ends and a lot of time spent mapping and logging everything, LeAnn finally found a tube with an old vent seal. It could only be accessed from the inside and did not have an airlock. It was meant for maintenance after a feeder tube was blocked off. But none of its feeder tubes had shut-off mechanisms. They had probably been removed when the Telfer tubes were abandoned.

That meant they had to install a temporary airlock. Getting one up there without anyone noticing was one of the premiere achievements of Ibrahima's career, if you believed her. The only way she got it signed out was to run simulations in her lab. The Mechanics team would come to take it back in five days. They needed to be done and have it back in Ibrahima's lab by then.

A tortuous series of Telfer tubes led to the access valve. The secrecy of their activities was nearly compromised several times as teams got lost and showed up in places they had no easy explanation for being in.

Somehow, they avoided detection and got the airlock installed. But they only had two days left if they wanted the whole thing to remain secret. Ibrahima gave them a less than 50 percent chance of success. The Passives had the machine under constant surveillance. It would be quite a trick for Corge to be able to fire up the machine and send a signal without anyone seeing him. In which case, returning the temporary airlock was the least of their worries.

Corge insisted that, when the time came, only he would head to the surface. If caught, he would claim he was solely responsible. If pressed on how he carried a temporary airlock sphere five times his size and weighing hundreds of kilograms, he would say he tricked some team members into bringing it there for a simulation run. As unbelievable as even that might seem, if he stuck to it, they couldn't bring evidence against anyone else.

He could work the airlock alone, but LeAnn would have to show him how, so he didn't kill himself or leak air. She insisted on testing it unoccupied first. Which made him worry about the integrity of the seal.

"Why do an unmanned test? You're risking losing air and I won't even be in there. I could be suited up and ready and, if the test went well, head on out. We don't have much time to spare."

LeAnn threw her hands up. "Fine!" If there's a bad bolt that goes explosive and jets you into orbit, far be it from me to complain that I wasn't given time to test. If the whole thing catches fire and melts you down, I'm sure your burned corpse won't blame me, since you wanted to go in without proper safety procedures. Go ahead, Corge. You're probably right! You probably won't explode or burn or be ejected. There's only one way to tell. Oh. Wait. No, there are two ways to tell. One that doesn't involve risking your life and one that does. But I guess that first one is too tame for a celebrity like you!" She stormed off down the tunnel, leaving Corge with another vent technician who had been tuning up the airlock for the test.

The technician looked unsure what to do. "Do you want," he motioned at the door and stuttered, "to—to go?"

"No!" Corge shouted. "She's right. Hold the test. I'll get her back," and he stomped off after her.

He caught up with her at an intersection of three tubes.

"LeAnn, I'm sorry. We're all just worried—"

She turned, grabbed him and kissed him hard. Taken by surprise, he did nothing in reaction because his body had taken over, and he was kissing her back just as hard. His hands began to do things on their own.

Corge decided that, as much as he seemed to enjoy this, it wasn't the proper time or place. As if having exactly the same thought at the same time, LeAnn pushed him back just as Corge was pushing her away.

"I just wanted to say I'm sorry," Corge heard himself say.

"Stop being sorry, you reclamation bin. I'm worried about you, too. Let me do my job!"

She stomped past him, but he decided he needed a little more clarification on what just happened. He gently grabbed her arm.

"I liked that, LeAnn. But I'm not sure what you meant by it."

She turned and smiled. "Always thinking too much, Corge. I think it's pretty clear what I meant by it. And while the timing may or may not have been the most romantic, I couldn't bear the thought of not getting a chance again. And that thought was distracting me. So. Thanks. It'll help me focus. Try not to ponder too much what any of this means until you get back, OK?"

She laughed at his stunned expression. "I realize that, with you, that's a little like asking you not to take up space. But try. Just for me. And I promise, when you come back in from the cold, we can approach the subject again in private."

Then he was straight blushing as she left him alone by the three openings.

CHAPTER 15

Ibrahima risked coming down into the tunnels to see Corge off. Corge stood near the airlock sphere, suited up and preparing for his walk on the surface. Chi-lin was checking off protocols while LeAnn fussed with Corge's suit. A few other technicians finished their last bits of prep on the sphere.

"You're 100 percent practiced and ready to do this fast, right Corge?"

"At least five nines Ibrahima," he responded with a smirk.

"You're actually getting a bit saucy. LeAnn must be rubbing off on you."

LeAnn choked a bit at this phrasing.

"Great!" Ibrahima declared clapping her hands together. "We'll get out of here so you can get to work. Give us about 20 minutes to get back into areas of plausible deniability. Then have at it."

"It'll take me about that long to get everything double-checked and ready to go," said Corge.

Ibrahima shook his hand, wished him good luck and then headed off.

Chi-lin gave him a hug. "You're going to be fine," she said.

"Thanks to you, Chi-lin. You were perfect." Chi-lin nodded and dropped her eyes at the compliment, then turned to follow Ibrahima. A few more technicians shook hands, patted him on the back and shared some last jokes. Finally, only LeAnn was left.

"I want to insist on staying," she said. "You need backup. But I know you won't have it," she held her hand up to stop his objection. "So go. And we have a date when you get back." She leaned in and gave him a light kiss on the lips and then left.

He was finally alone. He climbed into the airlock and shut the inward door. He sealed his suit by putting on his helmet and began the process of cycling the air out of the lock and back into the vent behind him. He went through all the double-checks for lock integrity and good seals with the older vent valve he would be pushing out of the way.

"Channel 5 test. Testing for observation mission tomorrow. Channel clear?" Chi-lin's voice came through the suit com.

"Clear, Chi-lin. Test out."

They would not communicate much during the mission unless he needed emergency help. Any Passives listening in would hear a small amount of normal chatter for a channel being set up for a very mundane observation mission on the surface.

The 20 minutes passed quickly, and before he knew it, Corge was on the surface. He had so much routine to deal with that he hadn't been nervous until he was about to take this first step up and out. He bent for the little jump he would need to make to get out of the angle of the tunnel when he realized he had almost left the case with his materials behind.

The case had the codes he recovered from the manual page. He had practiced a million times on the simulator, but if he ran into any snags, he wanted all that information at the ready.

His first job was to sneak up behind the machine without being seen. The Passives were observing the perimeter from the main surface observation area. The machine wasn't easily visible from there, but they had set up telescopes and cameras to watch the area. They didn't expect anyone to go to the trouble of sneaking around behind it. In fact, not being aware of the Telfer tubes, they didn't know anyone could.

The idea was to get to the machine unobserved, access the input mechanism without being noticed, enter the code, fire it up, and then dash back. If observers noticed anything, it would be the rising antenna, not Corge.

He got to the machine and clicked "open" on his coms three times to signal he'd made it.

"Channel 6 clear," he heard Chi-lin say. "Oops, crap. Wrong channel. Sorry, anybody listening!"

That confirmed to Corge that there was no indication anybody had seen him. Chi-lin was at the observer deck ostensibly preparing for a few upcoming missions while checking the reactions of observers. If anybody heard her signal, they would assume that old Chi-lin was messing something up again.

Now came the rough part. Corge inched around the side of the machine to the control screens. Ibrahima had drilled into him that if anybody saw him at that point, there wasn't anything they or he could do, so he shouldn't waste time looking around.

He resisted the urge to look and bent to the task, navigating through the selections and entering the codes. He could have easily left the case behind. He knew every step from memory and had no problems. He felt a thrill when he saw the diagram showing the signal being sent to the repeater box that would boost the message and send it to Earth.

His excitement almost overwhelmed him when the destination map came up showing a desert outside LA that must be SLC and a destination where New York once had been and might still be.

"Here goes nothing," he whispered to himself and entered into the screen, "CIT32 Active, NYC acknowledge. Comm REQ."

He pressed the screen to send it and let out the biggest sigh of relief in his life, feeling a big grin come on his face. Ibrahima had warned him to work fast and unemotionally, but he couldn't help it. He'd just sent a signal to Earth. He would wonder later if it was that moment that busted him. His com crackled to life.

"This channel isn't clear anymore. Repeat, not clear!' It was Chi-lin still in code but clearly alarmed. Someone suspected something. She would have requested the channel be shut down if they had seen him. He began to inch back around the machine to the place where his path back to the tunnel could not be observed. As he disappeared from view, he saw a few men in pressure suits walking toward the machine.

Every impulse in his body told him to run but he had to resist. If he ran, he not only risked propelling himself too far into the air and being seen, but also kicking up a lot of dust. If those people heading this way suspected something, they would look for telltale dust. He didn't dare look back for fear of wasting time. He marched determinedly straight toward the tunnel entrance.

He got back to the vent and started to crawl inside, finally letting himself turn and look behind him as he climbed in. He squealed to see three people reaching out to grab him. How did they get there so fast? They must have seen his dust after all and run after him. Why hadn't Chi-lin warned him?

"Come with us, Corge. You're charged with breaking the will of the Assembly and risking the well-being of the station."

Corge slumped. Nobody got the death penalty on Armstrong anymore, but that charge, if proven, would be as close to it as possible. They marched him back across the surface to the observation area. As they dragged him through the official airlock, he saw Chi-lin arguing with some official observers. No wonder she hadn't warned him—she'd been trying to keep them off her own back without revealing him. To her credit, she managed to look surprised as they pulled him past her. Or maybe she really was.

CAPITULUM 8

Dabashi stood with one hand on the Sculpture, staring out into nothing. He hadn't noticed Guteerez come in. Guteerez coughed politely.

"Oh. What?" Dabashi said, startled out of his reverie. "I'm sorry Guteerez. I didn't hear you come in."

"Quite all right, Dabashi. Any word?"

"No, none. He's not in any of the expected places. Not unlike him to disappear, of course, the vagrant. But very unlike him to disappear so completely and for so long."

At first, they had treated Michael's disappearance as an expected bit of moodiness. He had a record of such behavior. This would not help further his career, but nobody seriously worried about it. Instead, they prepared a harsh scolding. When it extended into days, though, some of the Superiors really did worry.

"Well, I'm sure he'll turn up. There's no reason to expect the Heretics would be interested in him or that he'd run off to join them. At least no serious reason I can think of," Guteerez looked at Dabashi with an odd expression.

"Oh stop that. Of course not. As much as I dislike the boy sometimes, I wouldn't peg him for a conspirator or an agent or any such thing. It has to be the work on the Sculpture." Dabashi looked away as soon as he said it.

"Why the Sculpture? Historical work seems rather predictable and safe," Guteerez probed.

"I'd rather not talk about it if it's all the same to you," Dabashi sniped.

Guteerez was about to try to draw Dabashi out on this point when the Sculpture antenna extended. Dabashi's face turned pale.

"What did you do?" Guteerez gasped, even though Dabashi was nowhere near the control box.

"Nothing," he whispered.

The Sculpture made more movements and noises.

"What is it doing?" Guteerez asked, dumbfounded.

"If I'm right," Dabashi said carefully, moving to the control box, "it's receiving a message."

"From where?!" Guteerez sounded uncharacteristically angry. "Is this Michael's doing?"

Dabashi stopped looking at the control box and stared. "Not likely at all." He paused, pondering Guteerez as if for the first time, and then went back to the box.

Guteerez gathered his robe around him and hurried around to peer over Dabashi's shoulder.

"How can you know?" he asked Dabashi.

"I just do," Dabashi snapped.

"Not good enough this time, Dabashi," Guteerez said with the undertone of a threat. "The other Superiors know you're hiding information. We all hide a little, but you can't hide something this big."

"I do what I must and what I'm sworn," Dabashi said, paraphrasing an Authority oath. "Do NOT challenge me, Guteerez."

Dabashi did not look up from the control box. Guteerez continued trying to see what Dabashi was doing.

"Fine. We'll talk about it later. What is happening to the Sculpture?" The antenna finished moving and a large number of symbols filled the control box. "Is that the message?"

"I believe so," Dabashi spoke slowly and carefully. He made a few selections and the characters disappeared.

"What did you do?!" Guteerez almost screamed. "Bring it back."

"It's saved," Dabashi said, refusing to say more.

"Dabashi, you can't behave like this and expect no repercussions. When I tell the Superiors of what you have done, the highest levels of the Authority—"

"You will do no such thing."

Guteerez laughed. "Won't I? And what leverage do you presume to have to stop me?" He let his expression soften. "Dabashi. My friend. This is not what Superiors do. We should work together. I'm sure if there's a good reason to go carefully, I can be made to see it and even agree. No?"

"No," Dabashi stated firmly.

"Why?" Guteerez snapped.

"I cannot say."

Guteerez sighed. "Well then what can you say? Let's start there." Guteerez seemed to have gained control of his emotions.

Dabashi clearly didn't like this line of questioning. "I'd rather say nothing than say too much."

"It's me, Dabashi. You can trust me. Don't tell me too much, but tell me something. Anything I can use to keep the other Superiors off your back." He was using the calm manipulation that always worked for him. "This won't stay secret. And when it becomes known, we'll need an explanation. You know that."

Dabashi paused but finally came to a decision. "Here is what I believe I can tell you." He spoke slowly and methodically, measuring every word to see if it said too much in the telling. "A message has just been received. I suspect I know where it is from, but I cannot say for sure and therefore cannot tell you my suspicion. If it is as I believe, it may be of historic significance and release me from my secrets. However, I cannot read what the message says at this time."

Guteerez nodded. "That is an acceptable answer, Dabashi. See? Things don't have to be so hard. So. Why can't you read the message?"

"It is coded."

Guteerez looked very odd at this revelation. "Do you—do you think Michael could decode it?"

"Most likely."

"Then we must find him."

"Immediately," Dabashi said, indicating the talk was at an end and sweeping past Guteerez to leave.

Guteerez stayed behind, staring. He tried without success to get the control box to reveal the message, but Dabashi had locked it away somehow. Guteerez pounded his fist on the box and stomped out.

CAPITULUM 9

Superior Murreket was expecting Dabashi. Murreket kept his chambers in an ancient restaurant several meters away from the Complex and the Citadel. He was not the eldest member of the Authority, but he was its eldest Superior. He had often declined promotion from Superior into the ruling councils. Few knew his reasons. Only Dabashi knew his true reason. And only Murreket knew Dabashi's secret.

"It may have begun," Dabashi said, without prologue or greeting, and sat down.

Murreket only grunted. "Our families have heard that before."

"The antenna deployed."

At this, Murreket raised an eyebrow as he gazed down on Dabashi. "Is that so? Well, you may be right."

"And a message was received. But I cannot read it. Monk Michael seems to have cracked the encryption, but he did not tell anyone how. Only he can read the message with any kind of speed, and speed is of the essence here, if my hopes are true."

Murreket nodded. "It is what my family protects," he said. "The means to speed."

"Do you know where Michael is?" Dabashi asked hopefully, half rising though still scowling.

Murreket got up and began to pace. "I may. As you know, we watch as you listen. I have not taken action. But our eyes saw a man in the guise of a Monk taken through the wilderness. It may be Michael."

"Is it Jackson? It sounds like Jackson and his precious wonders. Is it him?" Dabashi asked, sneering.

"It was. But the Monk was taken from him. Jackson is dead."

"Don't hold back, man, where is he?!" Dabashi stood, demanding.

"Do not presume to know all my secrets, Dabashi." He motioned for Dabashi to retake his seat. "I will tell you what I see the way you tell me what you hear—" he paused, "when you can."

Dabashi nodded. "Fine, fine. What can you tell me of what you've seen, then?"

Murreket laughed. "Michael, if it is truly Michael, was taken by men that fit the description of Chao's legion." Dabashi's mouth dropped open. Murreket held up a hand. "But the prisoner is not dead. As far as we have seen, he is alive and being fed. Someone is paying Chao with Authority gold. If that is not Michael, a rescue could undo all involved. If it is really Michael, a rescue would risk Chao's ire. The Authority would deny everything."

"How sure are you that it is Michael, then?" Dabashi asked.

Murreket thought long and hard about this. "Seventy-three percent."

Dabashi laughed. "You are very precise. That percentage is good enough for me to risk it. Especially in this case. How about you?"

"Yes," Murreket nodded. "I believe so. But discretion is still advised. So I would say we do not ask for outside help. We go with trusted sources."

"You know I have none," Dabashi stated flatly.

"You are wrong," Murreket chided. "You know me. And fortunately for you, I know several."

Dabashi smiled. "Of course."

"Come, we'll start at once. As you say, time is essential in this case."

CHAPTER 16

Armstrong rarely held trials. The station didn't have formal courts before Disconnection. Since then, society was so closely monitored with such willing acceptance from its citizens that disputes were rare.

But they did happen. So a small court met once a week for common disputes. Larger violations happened so rarely that only the full Assembly had the authority to hear them. In some of those rare cases, it had appointed a committee to hear the case and refer its judgment to the full Assembly for ratification.

Only once, in the case of poor Schmitz Tripathi, had a verdict been put to a vote of all station citizens. The Passives demanded this extraordinary measure in Corge's case, but the motion was defeated. Of course, if enough citizens signed a petition, it could be put to a vote anyway. The Passives were actively pursuing this but found the necessary number of signatures hard to reach.

In the meantime, Serafina efficiently pushed ahead with a trial in the Assembly. Unlike the historical courts of Earth, Lunar justice was swift. There was no weeks-long presentation of the evidence in front of a jury with chances for lawyers to twist words and sway opinions.

In a world used to weighing the urgency of even the most banal decision against its decades-long effect on survival, there was no time to waste words.

Charges were laid by accusers, who were, in this case, several of the Passives. Accusers and defense put forth facts that could either be disputed or not. The presiding judge would question the accused—in this case, Corge. In the case of an Assembly trial, it was usual for the Assembly leader to pose the questions as submitted by the body, therefore Serafina would interrogate him.

Witnesses would only be called if disputed facts were considered vital by the judge or the majority of Assembly members. The accused, or a representative, would have the right to speak, and a member of the harmed party would speak last. A verdict would be reached after a short recess using "The Chart."

Before Disconnection, in the leisurely golden age of the 'Delians, Nathaniel Kamel, a judicial scholar from the Dhaka Citadel, created an algorithm that could try any case objectively and come to a decision. It took the form of a flow chart of questions with answers provided by the accused, the accuser, or drawn from the evidence. It had never been used in 'Delian times partly because crime was so low and partly because of objections that it allowed no room for nuance. It worked too well at avoiding prejudicial answers, or at least accounting for them, and left no room for compassion. Kamel considered these objections a validation of his work.

Armstrong had needed swift justice after Disconnection and became the first society to implement Kamel's algorithm with much success. The speed of justice in Armstrong's small court was entirely attributed to it. Everyone in Armstrong had run up against The Chart at some time, even if for something as small as a behavior fine or a student evasion charge.

When the Assembly met, the system had to be adapted because the flow chart was meant for a single judge. Kamel had calibrated it to adapt to even the judge's biases. Even so, the Assembly voted on every response in aggregate, which meant that Kamel's system adapted to the biases of the Assembly as a whole. This slowed the process a bit and wasn't strictly necessary, but it prevented the urge for appeals by opposing factions.

Corge took comfort in knowing it was one thing the Passives couldn't manipulate.

On the way to the trial, Corge saw something he'd never seen on the station before. Civil unrest. While homemade signs would have been considered a waste of resources, the Passives had commandeered light readouts that they had reprogrammed from saying things like "Temporarily Closed" to things like "Stop the Madness."

A group of Corge's supporters, whom he barely knew, confronted several of the sign holders yelling slogans like "No Passive coup!" He didn't have any idea what that meant. Ibrahima had visited him overnight to prepare his defense and made some offhand comments about conspiracy charges against Assembly members. It looked like the idea had caught the public's imagination.

"I thought you said the idea of conspiracy charges was a crock?" Corge said to Ibrahima as they walked to the Assembly Room. Several of the crowd noticed him and began to boo and cheer depending on their persuasion.

"I never said it was a crock. I said it wouldn't happen," Ibrahima answered. Corge couldn't tell if her look was irritation or worry. "Apparently, word got out." She looked back at the crowd and then grabbed Corge's arm and pulled him in close. "We'll use this," she whispered.

Corge wondered how many conspiracies there might be.

The presentation of evidence was not controversial in the least. Ibrahima followed the plan. She asserted that Corge, on his own volition, had secretly decided to access the machine. He had sent a message and subsequently provided details of the method he used and the message he sent, as a show of good faith.

A very weak attempt was made to accuse Chi-lin as well, but the algorithm kicked out her line of questioning when it determined there was no evidence of complicity. It was deemed a waste of time and it was dropped. Corge could see the look of relief on her face.

The early questions had simple answers. They involved clarification of facts. Most facts were stipulated, so this part went fast. Corge answered the questions on his motivation by referring to the aims and goals of Armstrong, all of which referenced reconnecting with Earth.

Serafina asked each question with an even, emotionless tone. Her tone didn't change as she asked the last and hardest questions, the ones Corge had feared.

"Can you say with certainty that sending the message will not result in social damage to Armstrong?" she asked.

It was a trick question. If he answered yes, the algorithm would point to conflicting evidence from the Passives delay vote. If he answered no, it would point to a charge of "knowing risk" and taking that risk without authorization.

"Indeterminate," he said, as practiced. Serafina looked up. This was a valid response for the flow chart but one rarely used, mostly out of ignorance. Also, if a witness was discovered to be using it to avoid a known, they could be charged with contempt.

Corge thought he saw a smile creep onto Serafina's face for a split second as he answered. He definitely saw several scowls from members of the Passives. You could only get away with "indeterminate" if the answer to the question was in legitimate debate.

The Passives whole justification for delay was that doubt, so the algorithm would see the Passives' stance as support for Corge's answer.

"Did you receive authorization to enter the message?" Serafina asked. This one was unavoidable. If he said Ibrahima had authorized him, he would be admitting Ibrahima had directly violated the Assembly's orders and she would go on trial.

"No," Corge said. The Passives looked satisfied.

"Our final question, Corge," Serafina said dispassionately. "Have you incited unrest, either purposefully or not, by the sending of your message?"

They had not practiced this one. Unrest had not been entered into evidence. Corge felt like this was an evidentiary question, not an opinion or personal-knowledge question. He wanted Ibrahima to object, but there were no objections in Armstrong courts. The algorithm allowed the question, and it must be answered. This was not the movies.

He certainly hadn't purposefully incited riots. He thought hard. Why would the algorithm allow this question? The Passives wanted him to admit that sending the message had caused the protests outside and destabilized the base. But why? Because they couldn't enter it as evidence for some reason? But if the algorithm let it through, it saw his subjective answer as relevant.

Ibrahima was staring holes in him and Serafina looked as if she was about to hurry him on. He was required to answer each question promptly.

"No," he said to audible gasps. It wasn't a lie either. He knew the protests were not because of him. He knew the contents of his message—and he was a Generalist in Observation. The algorithm let him serve as his own expert witness. The protests were caused by the Passives. Granted, that was directly in response to the message, but if the Psychology team was asked to evaluate, they would find it was incited by the Passives' resistance to the project, not by Corge's actions.

"Thank you, Corge. Will you speak for yourself or will your representative?"

Corge nodded toward Ibrahima, who stood. She gave a brief, impassioned speech about the need for the message, criticizing the meddling meant to prevent it, and she explained how Corge could not be faulted for seeing the importance of it. She got to the conclusion they had rehearsed.

"The reasons for delay were flimsy and Corge knew that. At worst, he should be chided for undue haste. But the project was underway and he did exactly what the project would have done eventually anyway. Review the evidence of possible harm, and you'll see I'm right." She was supposed to stop there but didn't. "You heard Corge. Those protests outside were not caused by the message. Resistance to the project caused them. That resistance has destabilized us, not this man. Corge may have saved the station by forcing the issue before it got out of control. Thank you."

Ibrahima sat down, turned to Corge and made the gesture of thumb and pinky touching above and below the heart that meant "good luck."

Serafina adjourned the Assembly for deliberations. Some very polite security men led Corge to a waiting room where they made sure he was comfortable—and made sure he didn't go anywhere. Prisoners couldn't really go anywhere on Armstrong anyway, so it wasn't a very oppressive procedure. Corge ordered some coffee.

CAPITULUM 10

Michael decided long ago he would never give in. The people who did this deserved nothing from him. He knew someone else could possibly decipher the encryption and use the Sculpture, but he would not make it easy. He would not give in. But he would give up. Most sessions lately took him to the brink of his will to live. He had managed to fight against going over that brink. This time he decided not to fight. When he felt himself slipping away, he would let go. He smiled at the idea of depriving Chao of his answers.

He heard footsteps down the hall. He didn't recognize them. That almost never happened. He knew footsteps and smells. Every once in a while, a new person assisted in giving him his small amounts of water and food. Even then, he always recognized one of the people. He assumed they wouldn't let a new person go to him unaccompanied.

He couldn't see much anymore, so sounds and smells were all he had. Sounds were more pleasant, so he focused on them. As the footsteps drew near, the smell arrested his senses anyway. It was new. No wonder he couldn't ignore it. It wasn't just the smell of a new person; it was the smell of an outsider. Different clothes, steeped in different scents, not cloaked in the background stench of whatever place this was.

Figures loomed in front of him, blocking the light.

"Citadel's grace, is that Michael?" a voice said. It sounded familiar. He croaked something meant to be the word "yes," but it came out as a thin groan. He tried to nod his head. He couldn't tell if he succeeded.

"Cut him down carefully," the familiar voice said. A pungent smell filled his nose as someone moved in close to release him from his binds. It smelled like the Complex. Memories of his time there flooded back. He had lately tried to avoid thinking of the place as he let go all hope of returning.

He felt the binds release. He'd forgotten all about them. A sense of up returned as he fell forward. He knew distantly that he once was capable of moving on his own, but he'd forgotten how. He continued to fall and relished the feeling of motion and the breeze against his skin. It was luscious. The pungent-smelling person caught him and the breeze stopped.

The person set him gently down on the dirt floor and leaned him against the wall. The other person with the familiar voice leaned in close and said, "Drink this," and dribbled a ridiculous amount of water across Michael's mouth. The women who usually brought him water knew he could not take in that much. The water almost drowned him. He spluttered and spat, but some of it still made it into his throat. It was still too much. It turned to nausea in his stomach and he vomited.

"Go slow," the pungent person said. "He's not used to anything decent, I imagine."

"Of course. Sorry, Michael. We're going to get you out of here. If it makes you feel any—well—just know, the people who did this to you have been punished." The voice paused. Michael could tell he was being looked at. "Maybe not enough."

The familiar voice carried on, discussing how best to get Michael out of there. While they talked, Michael floated in a haze of pain and disbelief. He knew that voice. Brief images of the person flashed through Michael's mind.

It wasn't a good memory. It made him wary. Yet that voice treated him so gently and spoke so softly to him now. Forget that, the voice was rescuing him. Or was it? How could he be sure? Perhaps it was some new trick. He cowered back and pulled away as they tried to lift him.

His resistance did not seem to bother them much. He was too weak. They barely seemed to notice.

"It's OK, Michael. We're taking you back to the Complex where you'll be safe. It's me. Dabashi."

Michael screamed. In his mind, he screamed. In reality, it was a thin, keening whine.

"Stop. Stop. Stop," Dabashi snapped. Michael stopped the whine. The other man stopped moving Michael. "Michael. I know what you must think of me. In fact, now that I think about it, I wouldn't be surprised if you suspected me of arranging all this.

"Know this, Michael. I will never ask you for anything related to it. Not an ounce of information. Because I know more about it than you. You know what I mean. My attitude before was because I was afraid you would find out too much. I knew, in general, bad things could happen. I never dreamed someone would do this to you. I'm intensely sorry I let you proceed. I wish I'd been firmer. But whoever hired that man out there to do this to you must pay. And I will help you from now on. Not by asking anything of you, but by putting myself at your service."

Dabashi laid a hand gingerly on Michael's shoulder. "You don't have to say anything. Just let Acolyte Kangani lift you into the cart. Then you can rest. Although if you're awake enough, there's something I think you'll want to see on the way out."

It was too much for Michael to comprehend at once. Much too much and much too fast. But he got the general idea that Dabashi was there to help and that Dabashi would not ask him for anything. And an absence of questions is what Michael wanted right then more than anything. He relaxed a bit, and as much as his weakened body would allow, he helped get himself into the cart.

Acolyte Kangani pushed the cart up a series of ramps in what looked to Michael like a dark tunnel. Later, he couldn't be sure what it was, and he had no desire to discuss it with Dabashi or Kangani to find out. He never wanted to speak of that place again.

The ramp opened into a great, wide room with stone walls and a roaring fireplace. Along one wall sat the women who had helped feed and water him. He recognized their smell. He motioned for Kangani to stop near them. His sight had cleared a little, or maybe there was just more light in the room. He could almost make out their shapes.

"Thank you," he managed to gasp. The women moved but he could not tell in what way. Kangani leaned down and whispered, "They welcome you," and began rolling the cart forward again. Near the exit door, Dabashi stood next to a table on which Chao was strapped down. Michael knew that smell too. He also knew another smell and grimaced. It was the smell of burning flesh. This time, not his own.

Dabashi explained. "We have encased his hands in lead. He can, with great effort, remove them over time, but he will never have proper use of them again. Which means he can never repeat what he did to you.

Michael felt sorry. He certainly hated Chao. He certainly did not wish him well. But he felt it was improper to inflict same for same. He wondered if this didn't somehow justify Chao's treatment of

Michael in the end. But he only nodded as they passed out of the room.

CHAPTER 17

After a sleepless night and isolation from everyone, including Ibrahima, Corge found himself seated a few painful seats away from LeAnn who could only smile and wave to him. Ibrahima finally got permission to approach a few minutes before sentencing.

"It's going to be well," she said but did not look convincing.

"Then why did it take so long?" Corge hissed.

"That's a good sign," she said.

"Ibrahima, that's the kind of thing people say when the ventilator in the café fails on your wedding day. Or when a baby is born and gets black tongue on the first day. It's whistling in the dark."

She scowled at him. "I don't say that kind of reclamation paste. You know that." She lowered her voice to whisper and leaned in. "I'm saying—because a certain leader of the Assembly told me the Passives tried every procedural trick in the book, which only strengthened the opinion of the rest of the Assembly—that you are not considered the threat."

She leaned back and raised an eyebrow. "Now shut up before somebody hears that and decides to change their mind at the last minute."

Before Corge could respond, Serafina called for the chamber to settle and opened the proceedings. It was time for the verdict.

"Corge. The Assembly has considered the facts of the evidence. We have considered the logic of the questioning. And we have considered the pleas of your advocate.

"The Assembly finds you guilty of defying orders and assigns you to one year remedial Utility work under the Ventilation team, led by Specialist LeAnn."

Corge fought extremely hard not to laugh at this nonsentence. He admired how Serafina didn't crack a smile. It was certainly a punishment in one sense. He hated vent work, of course. But he thought an excuse to be near LeAnn for a year was probably worth it.

Serafina resumed. "The Assembly finds you guilty of property destruction in a minor and reclaimable amount. Your net rating will be reduced by the submitted amount."

So fewer coffees in the café for a while.

"And finally, the Assembly finds you not guilty of any charges of endangerment to the station or its civilization, in summary. Those charges and any like them related to this incident, now or in the future, are hereby dismissed."

He had been warned not to cheer, but he found it difficult. He had not only gotten off the serious charges but was indemnified against any new accusations the Passives could come up with. They had seriously messed up their strategy.

"You will be released without prejudice, assigned to LeAnn's Vent team and suffer the immediate deduction of 1005 points from your net rating." Here she turned to the Assembly and said, "Are there any objections to the sentencing as read?"

Aside from a few grumpy looks from some well-known Passives, there was no reaction.

"The sentence has been read and sustained. You are free to go, Corge." Here Serafina allowed herself the briefest of smiles as she nodded to him.

Ibrahima tried to shake his hand, but he found himself hugging LeAnn before he could think.

"You look horrible," she said, grinning madly after she let him go.

Ibrahima finally got close enough to shake his hand and said, "Get some sleep. Now. We'll talk about all this afterward. And good job."

"I didn't do much except stand there and be accused," Corge said.

"Some of the bravest men in history could say the same," Ibrahima said seriously. She patted him on the shoulder and walked away.

LeAnn took his hand and led him out of the chamber. They passed many smiling faces and received more than a few happy greetings, but people gave him his space as well. Partly, it was the respectful community culture of Armstrong. Partly, it was LeAnn.

When they got to Corge's bunk, she helped him into bed. He hadn't realized how exhausted he was until he lay down. He tried to pull her in with him, but she wouldn't let him.

"Sleep, celebrity. I'll check in on you in a few hours."

She shut the bunk on him and he stared up at the wall, looking for sugar rock. It took him a moment to realize why he didn't see any. He was almost off to sleep, or possibly sound asleep and dreaming he was falling asleep, when the bunk chime rang.

He thought it must be LeAnn returning to tell him one last thing. He authed the door open and two men he couldn't recognize pulled him off his bunk. They wore helmets to disguise their faces.

"Corge. We know why and what. And you know why and what we wanted to stop you. It stops here. We'll be watching you."

One of the men pressed his palm firmly into Corge's gut. It wasn't a punch. Corge realized it was legally short of assault, a firm and extremely uncomfortable pat on the stomach. Even if caught on surveillance it would not be punishable.

"Got it?" They let him drop back on his bunk and left. Corge took a little longer to fall back asleep after that as he tried to figure out what they meant.

CAPITULUM 11

Michael took several weeks to recover. Even then it was not something he would call complete. He flinched at things. Things he felt sure were imaginary, just flutters in his peripheral vision. Yet other things that used to frighten him did not anymore. He used to try to avoid looks from the doctors. He didn't like the pressure of having to react.

Now he not only met their gaze but held it until they looked away. He took a perverse pleasure in staring them down.

When finally allowed out of bed, the first thing he wanted to do was get back to work on the Sculpture. Guteerez was more than happy to let him do so.

"We've missed you puttering about in there," the Superior told him when visiting one day in the infirmary. "The faster you're back, the better we'll all feel." Michael felt good seeing Guteerez's wide, welcoming smile again. As good as Dabashi had been in rescuing Michael, the man was hardly ever warm. Michael no longer feared Dabashi, but he wasn't sure he liked him. Intensely grateful, yes, but "like" might be a strong word for his emotions.

Guteerez, on the other hand, fell right back into Michael's good graces. The Superior visited him every day he was bedridden and even brought him small food items and tokens of entertainment to help him pass the time during his recovery. Rationally, Michael knew it was possible Guteerez was somehow involved in his torture. But he couldn't really make himself believe it. The man was too kind and too accommodating. Why have Michael captured and tortured when he could have probably talked Michael into showing the encryption codes just by being nice? Especially since Michael's experience had changed his mind completely on who to share information with.

Michael had learned at a dear price how to separate emotions and actions. He was willing to use the encryption codes for Dabashi but only in person with no one else present. Michael was steeled against sharing the codes with anyone else, even Guteerez.

The day finally came when he walked back into the Sculpture room in the Reliquary. It was mostly as he had left it. A few things had been moved about but not much. The control box screen was on a selection to start operating. Dabashi said he saved the message, but it took Michael a half a day to get back to the point where he knew how to work the control box well enough to find it.

At that point, he had to be careful. Dabashi had ordered him not to show the decrypted message to anyone. Dabashi didn't even want to see it. He insisted that nobody but Guteerez even knew one had been received.

"You will make absolutely certain nobody is coming, or I will interrupt you when you decrypt it," Dabashi had told him. You'll commit it to memory after decryption and then delete it. Do you understand? No one sees it. No one traces it. You tell it to no one."

Michael understood quite well.

He checked the hallway and saw nobody. He closed and barred the chamber door.

His hands shook and a tear rolled down his cheek as he executed the decryption. At first he wasn't sure it worked. The message didn't make sense. Was it more encryption? He didn't think so. He quickly memorized it. A selection existed to confirm receipt. Dabashi had said nothing about that. Michael decided one more secret couldn't hurt anyone. So he selected yes. The antenna deployed briefly, and the machine worked for a brief moment. Then the antenna retracted and the box displayed confirmation that the receipt had been sent.

Michael erased all traces of the message, including the saved encrypted version. He heard footsteps. He backed out of the selections and raced to the door. He unbarred it moments before Guteerez opened it.

They both looked at each other, surprised.

"My dear, Michael! You startled me. Whatever is going on in here?"

Michael heard himself talking before he even thought what to say. "The door must have slipped closed. It gets so stuffy in here, I walked over to prop it back open right when you arrived," he found himself laughing, uncharacteristically bemused. "You startled me just as much or more. Come in, Superior."

Guteerez smiled but Michael thought he saw a hint of suspicion. "Did Dabashi tell you of what we found?"

We, eh? Michael thought. "Yes," he said out loud. I regret to say that the encryption has proved too difficult for me as yet."

A look of angry surprise flittered briefly across Guteerez's face. "Well that's too bad. Keep at it, my boy. I'm sure you'll get it. Am I right?" The barest hint of a threat threaded its way through those words.

Michael sighed. "Yes, of course. I just need awhile to get back up to speed on how this all works. I've forgotten so much," he paused and caught himself honestly beginning to cry a bit. And though it was not for show, he worked it anyway. "I've gone through so much."

Guteerez softened. "There, there, Michael. No rush. Do your best. If you need anything, you just tell me, OK?"

"Thank you, Superior," Michael said gratefully. "I think I'll take a break and get something to eat."

"Good idea," Guteerez said and hung back in the room. Michael was almost certain he knew why. But he wouldn't find anything. Hopefully the lack of the saved encrypted file wouldn't be obvious to Guteerez. But either way, who could he tell? He might suspect Dabashi as much as Michael.

Michael made certain he wasn't followed, passing through the dining area and picking up a small bit of bread. Then he went to Dabashi's private quarters. It was risky in some ways for a Monk of any kind to be seen visiting a Superior's nonwork room, but it was less likely to be observed.

Dabashi opened the door and hurried Michael in to close it behind him.

"Do you have it?" Dabashi asked.

Michael nodded. "I can't make sense of it but I have it. And I deleted all trace. Also—"

"What?" Dabashi almost yelled.

"I sent a confirmation of receipt."

"You what?!" Dabashi caught himself before raising his voice and converted it into a harsh whisper. "You ridiculous boy." But then his looked softened again. His gaze fell on Michael's scars. "That was wrong. Too many might notice. Not the people it was intended for up there, but others eavesdropping." Dabashi shook his head. "Well, they knew already, I suppose. Tell me the receipt does not include the original message."

"It does not."

Dabashi sighed. "Then let's have it."

"It makes no sense," Michael said.

"To you," Dabashi said impatiently. "Speak it."

"CIT32 Active, NYC acknowledge. Comm REQ."

Dabashi nodded. "Very good."

"Do you know what it means?" Michael asked.

"Yes."

"Tell me."

Dabashi shook his head.

"I bled for that message. Tell me," Michael demanded.

Dabashi raised his eyebrows. "I see. Too lazy to figure it out, I guess." Dabashi chuckled and went over to a side table and poured out two drinks of werewater. Michael almost declined. He didn't drink werewater and worried what it would do to him. But he took it graciously in the end. Dabashi toasted him. Michael took a small sip that burned his mouth.

"'Cit32' obviously means Citadel 32 or the Moon. 'Cit32 Active' means that the Citadel is active. Most likely, that means the machine, but if the machine is active, then people are too. 'NYC acknowledge' means they are asking for the New York Citadel to acknowledge the message. It was the customary way, in the Citadelian Age, to begin communication at a distance like this. 'Comm REQ' means communication requested. It means they aren't just sending us a note, they want to talk in real time," Dabashi took another sip. "That's all. A big, long line of gibberish that means, 'Hey, let's chat.'"

"So," Michael scowled, "how do we chat?"

Here Dabashi looked disappointed. "That is going to be difficult to do and keep secret. And even if it is possible, it's dangerous. I'm afraid this is a situation come too early. My family did not expect our society to still be in this state at this point. I'm not sure we're ready."

Michael heard the doubt. "But we have to talk with them! They're us. They survived. Think of all the knowledge and information they must have preserved."

"Exactly, Michael. Think of all that knowledge in the hands of someone like Chao or Jackson. Can you say we're ready, Michael? Can you?"

CHAPTER 18

Corge couldn't relax, especially with Chi-lin there. He tried to focus on the machine, but he kept looking over his shoulder expecting to see Passives coming for him. Every time he did, he saw Chi-lin instead and then had a whole other panic attack as he tried to remind himself that she was not, in fact, breaking the law and risking their discovery.

It would take some getting used to.

He stared out toward the area where the Telfer tube let him out on the surface. It was no wonder the tube hadn't been discovered. Dust covered it quickly with all the traffic in the area, and it was hidden in shadows anyway. Even a team that knew where it was needed him to come show them. He barely found it himself. The airlock cover seemed to disappear under the thinnest layer of anything.

"Corge, I know it's fun to reminisce, but I'm getting hungry," Chi-lin said through the com.

He laughed. "You can go without me Chi-lin. As much as my brain doesn't want to believe it, I don't think anyone's after me."

"Tell that to Ibrahima who will pass it along to the two guys who roughed you up in your bunk," she answered.

"They didn't rough me up." He wished he had never mentioned it. In the two weeks since the incident, he hadn't heard a peep out of the Passives. He decided to put all that out of his head and get back to the reason he was here. He actually got to investigate the entire machine interface this time, not just race to the send button. He was doing his job as an Observer. Ibrahima had hinted that a good report on this would make him a lock to become a Specialist in Observations.

He was capturing and documenting all the menu pages this time, hoping to recreate some kind of user manual. As he flipped back through the options to see if he missed any, he noticed a red indicator light in the messages menu. He was almost certain it hadn't been there before.

He checked his portable. An image he had just captured of that screen showed no red marker. He wasn't imagining it. Something had changed. He entered the messages section and let out a low whistle.

Next to the menu item for receipts, he saw the number one. There was a message.

"Chi-lin!" he yelled. "You must see this!" She didn't answer right away, but he couldn't wait. He selected the menu item and there in the Receipts screen was the following: "CIT32 Message Op Rec'd NYC - 1528030476."

The New York Citadel's machine had received the message and an operator had authorized a return receipt. Corge didn't care what kind of operator—human, mutant or robot—it was not an automatic response. Something down there had looked at the message and acknowledged it. He frantically rechecked to make sure a follow-up incoming message had not been received, but there was nothing there.

Still he let out a wild cry of "Whooop!" and turned to tell Chi-lin. She wasn't there.

Instead, two figures in suits grabbed him and leaned in to touch their helmets to his. When they did, he noticed Chi-lin on the ground, motionless.

Their voices came through the helmets, not through the coms, weak and thin but menacing.

"You didn't see anything, Corge. You got that?"

Corge didn't say anything.

"It won't be violence we use against you. You know that. But your hard-earned reputation will bleed away. Stories about your faults and fetishes will circulate. People always want to believe that heroes have a dark side. We'll make yours very dark and very believable. You won't make Specialist. You won't stay a Generalist. You'll be lucky to avoid Tender. Tell me you understand."

"I do," said Chi-lin's voice over the coms. She had got up without any of them noticing and caught on to what was going on. "You're unstable elements threatening the community. Even if you weren't picking on one of my best friends in the whole station, I'd still want you busted down to Tender myself."

Before Corge knew what happened, and before she had even finished her speech, the two men were on the ground and she had their hands behind their backs.

"Where did you learn that?" Corge asked.

"I failed out of Security, remember? I learned a few things there."

"How did you hear them?"

"What do you mean, 'how'? Through your com. I thought it was smart you left it on!"

Corge realized he'd flicked it on to tell Chi-lin the good news and never turned it back off.

"Yeah, exactly! Glad you picked up on that."

Chi-lin laughed. "I'm an old hand at accidentally doing the right thing. Your secret's safe with me. I already messaged for someone to help take these two off our hands. Are you done?"

Corge began to whoop again. "Oh man, you don't even know yet. You are not going to believe this!"

CAPITULUM 12

Superior Murreket sat in the restaurant, a cup of something steaming in front of him as he reviewed some documents. He did not look up as Dabashi brought Michael in but merely waved for them to sit across the table from him.

"Superior Dabashi speaks well of you, Michael," Murreket said without looking up from his documents.

"Uh, thank you," Michael stammered.

Murreket looked up at Michael. "No need to thank me for his compliment. He has told you why you're here?"

Michael opened his mouth, but the Superior didn't give him the chance. "And you know the consequences if you speak of our meeting to anyone?"

Michael didn't respond this time and Murreket glared. "Well?"

"Superior Dabashi told me that if anyone asked, I should say that he was introducing me to you as a potential scribe."

Murreket nodded. "You're right, Dabashi. He doesn't appear to be much at first but he has a mind in him. Michael, what I'm about to tell you is dangerous for you to know. I would not burden you with it if it wasn't necessary and if you weren't already burdened with more dangerous information as it is.

"My family has guarded the annals of the 'Delians for time out of mind. We journeyed on foot from Ellay, through the museum city of San Francisco, across the great mountains, through the museum cities of Salt Lake, Danver, Santlewis, Clevund and all the way here, gathering what we could preserve.

"Many know this, but most misunderstand. We hold information that points to other information that would help unlock the true knowledge many hope would return civilization to its proper state. Many within the hierarchy want it to stay lost. No, Michael, not like the Heretics do. Rather, they feel we would be better to relearn it all ourselves. Others wish to control it to gain power. Those are the ones who took you. They believe the machine holds that information. They believe if there are people on the Moon that they should be brought back to give us the information. None of that should happen. We cannot allow it."

"Why?" Michael interrupted. Dabashi moved to chastise him, but Murreket raised a hand and an eyebrow simultaneously.

"It would be impudence if Michael did not know what he knows. But he does. Michael, the one principle my family knows directly is the principle of the ready society. When we, as a society, are capable of certain things and hold certain ideals in common, then we will be ready to restore the knowledge of the 'Delian Age. We are not ready. Not yet."

"So what do we do?" Michael asked. "Ignore the Moon?"

"For the moment, yes. What you have done has accelerated things a bit on their end, but we can maintain balance on ours. We have to let others here think the information has become irretrievable again. We have to let their agents see you destroy it. Or seem to."

"Agents? Guteerez?"

Dabashi spoke up. "We don't know. But we do know that what has played out in that room with the Sculpture has been discovered. Either it is monitored or Guteerez is their agent. Either way, he has to be dealt with, as he knows more than is good for him."

"Superior Dabashi has a plan," Murreket said. "Which I wholly endorse."

It took some doing, but Dabashi convinced Michael to play along with the scheme. They confronted Guteerez in the Reliquary and ushered him into the Sculpture room where Dabashi closed and barred the door.

Michael thought Guteerez showed a hint of fear, but he mostly looked curious.

"Michael has done a stupid thing," Dabashi declared, rounding on Guteerez then glaring at Michael.

"Whatever do you mean?" Guteerez protested. "Michael, is this true? What is it?"

"Tell him," Dabashi commanded in a furious tone. If Michael didn't know for sure this was the plan, he would have been convinced Dabashi wanted to kill him.

"I sent a receipt to the message."

Guteerez's eyes lit up at this. "So you decrypted the message!"

"No," Michael lied. "I don't know who it came from or why. I believe it may even be a bug. But I found the receipt menu and—I thought if I sent the receipt, they might send a response in clear text or something. I don't know."

"What if it's wilderness people?" Dabashi yelled. "What if it's Heretics, Michael?"

Guteerez looked thoroughly worried. "I'm sorry to say it, Michael, but he's right. It very well could draw unwanted attention to the Sculpture and the Complex. Yes, the Heretics know where we are, but they don't know we have a machine capable of signaling the Moon. If they did, it might stoke their fires to the level of days of old."

"Shut it down," Dabashi commanded.

Michael pleaded against the command and looked to Guteerez for help.

Guteerez just shook his head. "He's right, Michael. We can't risk it. Don't worry. We won't destroy the Sculpture. But I know you know how to disable it and you must do so. There can be no chance of another message slipping out or traced in any way by broadcasts or electrical usage. You can keep copies of the encrypted message and continue to work on it, of course."

"No," Dabashi snapped. "No records. No words. Nothing happened in here. He shuts it off. Guteerez, you and I make sure that antenna is sealed in for good and we speak no more of it ever."

Guteerez sighed. "I suppose."

This was too easy, Michael thought. He had expected Guteerez to put up a fight.

"Michael," Guteerez laid a hand on the Monk's shoulder. "It may have been wrong of us to let you keep at it, anyway. The forces that took you are known to me. Not by name but by their works. Had they known you made any progress, I can't say they wouldn't have tried again, and who knows what they would have done this time. Dabashi is hotheaded," here he looked slightly chiding at his fellow Superior. "But he has the right idea usually. Can you promise to put this behind you? I know how it must break your heart. It was your life. But it may *save* your life to abandon it now. You were not wise to send that receipt."

Michael felt that Guteerez was being honest. Whatever Dabashi suspected, and whatever secrets Guteerez hid, Michael found it hard to believe the Superior meant him any harm or could have had anything to do with the torture or kidnappings.

"You wanted this as much as me," Michael said almost as a question.

A tear came to Guteerez's eye. "Let's just say another young Monk spent a lot of time in this room and never got near to the secrets you've uncovered. If that Monk could see you now, he would be overjoyed. A real smile came to Guteerez's face.

Michael began to doubt. Was he doing the right thing? He still half suspected Guteerez was on the wrong side. How could he know for sure?

"You heard him," Dabashi said, snapping Michael out of his reverie. "Shut it down and speak no more of it. If anyone were to ask, we will say it simply stopped working on its own. Such are the mysteries of the Citadelian Age." It was a common enough occurrence with old things like this.

Michael slowly made the selections that leaked the power out of the machine. He felt the lack of its energy in the room. Dabashi climbed up on a chair and pulled out a vial of a thick, milky substance.

"Superior Guteerez, if you would be so kind as to grab that cloth over there and guard against spillage," Dabashi asked in his polite voice reserved for fellow Superiors.

With Guteerez's assistance, they used the substance to plug up the antenna hole.

"And that is that," Dabashi said, wiping his hands on the cloth with a grim air of finality.

"But we know so much more than we did," Guteerez said wistfully. "It's a shame we can't share it."

"We know they're there," Michael said. Guteerez gave him a questioning look and Dabashi just looked away.

"We know they're there," they all repeated.

CHAPTER 19

It was a ceremony. More than a ceremony, it was a blasted party. Almost everyone in Armstrong who didn't need to be inside the dome running the place gathered on the surface.

Serafina stood by the machine and blasted a message over the coms.

"This is an unusual use of surface resources today, as you all know." No one sent their laughter back over the coms but the nodding and bobbing helmets made their reaction clear.

"But it's an exceptional day. Against much undue resistance, and with a singleness of purpose, Specialist Corge successfully made contact with Earth and received a confirmation that the message was received. While we have not received a further response, the Assembly has unanimously authorized another message to be sent in clear text.

"We don't know what the state of the people in the New York Citadel is, or even if they are people. Possibly they could not encrypt our first message. With that in mind, our unencrypted message will read as follows. Corge?"

Corge switched on his com and his voice shook as he read. "Attention Earth, this is Moon Base Armstrong. We are alive. Please respond. Armstrong out."

A silent wave of clapping reached Corge's eyes, and he nodded. Serafina said nothing more but waved him back to the machine.

Corge approached and went through the same procedure he'd gone through when he sent the first message, this time turning off encryption.

However, when he got to the transmission screen, he received a punch in the gut. A red error warning existed where the transmission details should have been. Before, the NYC machine was listed as a destination. Now it gave him nothing. He tried several alternate ways, but they all read the same.

Finally he made it to a status screen he hadn't explored before and saw the code "NYC - Offline." He pounded a fist on the machine. He tried several other ways to get to a transmission screen but found nothing. From what he had learned, this meant someone, or something, had turned off the New York machine. It hadn't been damaged. He was certain. That was a different code. This was voluntary shut off. They'd received his message and their response was to turn the thing off? Had he scared them? How was that possible? He'd sent the simplest of machine messages. And yet he had tried everything. There was no way to escape it. New York didn't want to talk right now. He almost collapsed onto the machine when he remembered that most of Armstrong was watching.

He turned and saw them standing silently. Waiting. He couldn't see expressions. He couldn't tell their attitude. All helmets were turned toward him. Serafina, who was closest, just motioned toward her com button and pointed at him. This was his job.

He took a deep breath and pressed the button. "I'm sorry, everyone. The machine says NYC is offline. Maybe they had a malfunction and had to turn the machine off to repair it. But there's no doubt they turned it off. They got our message. Then they turned off their machine for some reason. I—" his throat caught. He could not let himself break down now. He had to take responsibility. What had they done? "I'm so sorry. There won't be any communication with Earth. Not today." He hung his helmet.

"It's OK," Serafina said, broadcasting to everyone. "We'll keep monitoring. Keep listening." Other helmets hung in sorrow and solidarity. No one spoke, but everyone moved forward. Corge thought they might try to rush him. His gut knotted up at the memory of the attack at his bunk.

But as they approached, they held out their gloved hands and either shook Corge's or patted him on the back, as if he were the one most affected by this, not their entire civilization.

They moved inside to Docking Bay, packed to the gills but eerily quiet. Not a full silence. Scattered whispers floated on top of it. But it was not the normal Docking Bay crowd buzz.

Serafina stood and began to speak, scattering the whispers into the corners. Only her voice remained.

"Today was a great disappointment. There is no doubt about that. We do ourselves and our descendants a disservice if we think otherwise. But it is not a failure. Progress is not linear. We ALL know that."

"Corge endangered us all," a voice shouted from below. A murmur followed it. The silence was ripped apart by it and the murmuring filled the new gap. Serafina looked toward the voice. Corge feared a riot might start. But then he listened to the murmurs.

"You're endangering us if you don't shut up."

"I don't think Corge shut off the machine on Earth, did he?"

"He's gangly but his arms aren't that long!" followed by a chuckle.

"Anybody speaks against Corge speaks against Armstrong, as far as I'm concerned."

More murmurs rose along the lines of these, at least those Corge could hear. No more Passives spoke.

"Quiet please," Serafina said gently, and the murmurs settled to the bottom of the silent room.

"We risk arrogance sometimes in estimating our own dangers. We risk foregoing actions we need to take. RISKS we need to take if we believe our own theories too strictly. Far from being a danger, this entire series of events has been a blessing for Armstrong. We risk stagnation just as much as chaos," a few gasps met this as it verged on sounding like the Heretics of the Disconnection age. "We need these kinds of unforeseen events to wake us up. Make us challenge our own beliefs and adjust them. Corge," she turned to look at him, "you have given us a great gift. I cede the remainder of my time to you. I know we didn't plan that and you're not prepared. That's exactly what we need from you. Unplanned and unprepared remarks. Armstrong, I give you Corge!"

Docking Bay's silence fled as a roar of approval chased it away. Corge climbed the stairs to the platform where Serafina spoke. He stood in the historic spot where Disconnection had been announced.

"She's not kidding. I have nothing planned and I don't know what to say," good-natured laughter kept the silence away and Corge fed off it. "This spot," he looked down at the platform. "I'd like to think today this spot changes for us. We think—most of us anyway—think of this spot as where Disconnection happened. Where it was announced. Starting today—" Was he really going to say this? Well Serafina had just given him license to say whatever he wanted. The crowd looked at him with a multitude of eager faces. "Starting today, I'd like us to think of it as a place where someday Reconnection will happen. Let's not be afraid. This was for all of us.

"We know they have a working machine. We know they heard us. And as much as all of us would have liked a further response, we can all take one thing out of this—a precious thing that we weren't sure of before. Pass this along and pass it down. We know they're there."

The room erupted. He saw people pumping their fists in the air. He heard a chorus of voices chanting, "We know they're there."

Post Scriptum

Michael sat at a writing desk in the Complex's journalist wing. It had apparently been an actual news organization in ancient times. He had taken to writing bits of nonsense and poems, some rather dark, others light and fun, that were published as entertainments for the pleasure of the Complex.

Guteerez peeked in and greeted him. "What are you working on now, my fine poetic genius?" he kidded.

Michael grinned. "One that Dabashi is not going to like."

"Does he like any of them?"

Michael laughed. "I suppose not. But this one especially will drive him wild."

"Then I must hear it," Guteerez commanded in a mock martial tone.

In truth, Michael had already read it to Dabashi who said, "It's quite nice. Of course I'll have to pretend to hate it. Try not to take it personally. But do read it to Guteerez before you publish. Just to be sure."

So Michael read it.

"Up on the Moon you cannot fall

Up on the Moon to wait in the hall

Up on the Moon untillen we call

Up on the Moon come back to us all."

Guteerez dabbed at his eye. "Very good, Michael. Nobody but us will know exactly why it's so good, of course, but good all the same. And you're right. Dabashi will hate it."

They both chuckled at the thought.

Epilogue

Decades later.

Ji lay on her back staring at the Moon. She picked this place because it was high up and far away from everyone. It had the majestic desolation and gigantic skeletons of buildings that Ellay had but without the crowds.

Stories of poisonous mutant animals kept the idle curious out of the Empire Desert. Around her sat miles of ruins, once homes and shops a long time ago. Most were just crumbling cement foundations now, harboring a few reptiles. Some of those were poisonous, she knew, but she doubted any were actually mutants.

When she heard the news earlier that day, she headed straight out to her favorite spot in the abandoned settlement of Ontreo. The building she climbed had resisted the crumbling and wreckage of time that had crumbled so many other ruins. Large, orange letters from the ancient alphabet still clung to the side. She translated them once but it made no sense to her. House Train Station? Something had definitely been lost in the translation.

Whatever it had been, it was now a solid steel structure that somehow hadn't rusted into collapse. She had grabbed a bag of M&M'S, hit the road and here she lay, staring up into the night sky.

She loved M&M'S. They gave her a sense of history. Few "brand names" had persisted over the centuries from pre-'Delian times. Many had disappeared in the 'Delian Age's sophistication and the following collapse, but M&M'S somehow had survived.

It was an affectation she knew. She loved the idea that she was somehow connected to the past, even if the connection was a spurious and intermittent usage of a name. M&M'S had changed much over the centuries. It was odd to her to think that the lightly candied pretzel bits, nuts and cherry balls she enjoyed were not at all what the snack had been like even 100 years ago. A historian claimed the original M&M'S had been hard candies with a bean paste inside. She wasn't sure she believed that, but she accepted that the brand hadn't always meant the food she loved now. And yet that was part of the reason she loved them. She felt like she was eating history.

The nostalgia brought back to her a poem she learned as a little girl.

Up on the Moon you cannot fall

Up on the Moon to wait in the hall

Up on the Moon untillen we call

Up on the Moon come back to us all.

She watched as the light of their capsule moved through the sky. Now they were coming back.

Printed in Great Britain
by Amazon.co.uk, Ltd.,
Marston Gate.